I0658719

SOMETHING

CHICK GALLIN

Olmstead Publishing
2013

Olmstead Publishing
Personalized, On Demand, Small Order Publishing
www.OlmsteadPublishing.com OlmsteadPublishing@USA.com

"Something" is a work of fiction, names, places and incidents are purely the imagination of the author. Any resemblance to actual persons, living or dead is entirely coincidental.

Table of Contents

A fog, a hometown hero, a motorcycle gang war, three veteran detectives in a small town, and the problems that have to be rectified before that town can be at peace again.

As Detective Ralph Bloom was saying to his partner Detective Alan Beckman, and Special FBI Agent Gina Grant. "Something very strange is happening in Arthur."

Dedication

This book is dedicated with love to my big brother Morty Gallin who was taken from us way too soon. You will be missed by all.

Acknowledgement

Thank you always for
your support my love,
my life, my wife.

Prologue

Lewis (Lew) Wallace had no idea just how many lives he had intercepted, nor did he know how many acts of his had stirred so many people to remember and marvel at his unselfish deeds.

The fact of the matter was that Lew did not even remember what he had done. It was as if it were someone else who had performed the sometimes-amazing feats.

Lew Wallace was the ultimate in unassuming. He went about his life and business doing things that he considered, just being a good person and neighbor.

He held no one in contempt. He was not jealous of anyone. He had loved only one person, besides his mother and father, and because he was an only child, he had no siblings with which to share this love.

His wife of twenty-five years had never seen a hostile or angry moment in their entire married life. He was so mild mannered that, at times, he seemed invisible. That is how innocuous he appeared.

However, many times in the recent past he had acted so out of character that even old friends, who had looked upon him as a hero, were surprised.

He had done something, something he did not even remember, something that would follow him until the day he would die, but he had no idea of what that something was.

All he knew was that people, people he did not even know, would stop him on the street, come up to him, wherever he was and shake his hand or slap him on the back, and thank him. At the bank or the supermarket, even in a darkened movie house people came up to thank him what he had did that was so great.

He would look at these people and wonder why they were all applauding an action of his. However, being the man he was, he took their good feelings in his modest stride, never asking why.

His wife was almost as unassuming as Lew and she would never ask him what he had done to bring about this sort of adoration. It was enough for her that everyone thought he was as wonderful as she did.

Lew worked as a clerk in the local sporting goods store, a nationwide franchise, a well-known store that carried every conceivable type of sports equipment. He was well versed in every aspect of every sport and could advise potential customers on the best and the least expensive gear needed for a particular sporting activity.

Lew had no expectations or desire to be anything more than he was, an assistant manager.

The position afforded him the latitude to make minor decisions and to escape the pressure of being in charge of the store and its employees.

He loved his job, and resisted every effort for promotion, but was always polite in his refusals. No one in the front office held these refusals against him and regarded him as a valuable asset to the company.

UNTIL!!! Until the day that changed things so drastically that they were stunned to disbelief. This man, who was such an anti-heroic choice, was suddenly being lauded for something he had done.

Chapter One

Lew found himself in the deepest fog he had ever seen. Nowhere that he had ever been, and that counted the four years spent in the U.S Air Force stationed overseas in Germany at Ramstein Air Force Base and close to the coast of England, had he ever experienced a fog this dense.

This fog clogged his throat with its thickness, forced his eyelids down, and put so much pressure on his ears and nose that he thought he would surely die from not enough oxygen if it did not let up.

It did not, and best of all he did not succumb. Somehow, he found the strength inside himself to slow down all his senses, and after the longest time, it seemed, in his life, he began to overcome all those feelings and breathed just a little easier.

He still could not see very well, but instead he felt a presence about him. It seemed to be leading him somewhere. Nothing he could do would take this feeling away, so he let it lead him unknowingly in the fog. The strangest part of it was that he was not afraid, feeling it was a good presence and he felt, rather knew, that no harm would come to him or anyone he loved.

The fog lasted a long time and as he looked at his watch, he saw it was late, almost morning. He wondered where the time had gone, and more so, wondered what he had done in all that time. He could not remember traveling any distance. It was as if he had merely been stumbling in the rich deep fog not knowing how far he had gone.

Chapter Two

His wife Linda, of 25 years, was quite used to his nighttime rambling. In fact, she attempted to follow him once when they had been married for only five years. She followed until she was certain he was not going off to see another woman, but seemed to be just roaming the streets. He met no one and no one appeared to accost him in any way, shape, or matter.

She marked this down as one of his idiosyncrasies and, being that he was a good and loving husband and an excellent provider, she decided to ignore those random roamings as just something he did.

It was not until something extraordinary occurred that she remembered that some of his outings took more than one day and sometimes more than a week. His business, not being his, did not suffer and the times away did not affect his position in the company, so nothing was ever said about his times off.

She knew that when she could not find him in her bed or anywhere in the house that wherever he had gone to had something to do with his mysterious outings. Never on his returns had he displayed any ill effects, on the contrary, he appeared to be more relaxed and happy. His moods for the next few days were more of a pleasure than before. Never had he shown even a modicum of anger and never had a harsh word or look at his wife, so his demeanor had not changed in any form.

Therefore, when Lew disappeared again she took it in stride and went about her daily ministrations without a second thought.

Chapter Three

Things had been unusually quiet at the squad room that housed the Homicide Division. The run of the mill street killings were recorded and found to be down 16 percent, which indicated that the mild weather was not conducive to violence of the homicide nature.

The two detectives that headed the division had between them twenty-five to thirty years of experience on the job.

Detective Ralph Bloom, the now Lieutenant of the squad, had been the lead detective on many cases, 90% of which he brought to a successful conclusion. Bloom was an unassuming man who did not display the usual animus against the criminals he arrested, in contrast with many of the long time cops who developed a hardness and anger towards the people who perpetrate crimes.

Ralph and his second in command, Detective Alan Beckman, had worked together for so many years they rather knew what the other was thinking. Alan was slightly more outgoing than his longtime partner was and, at times, displayed a quiet anger that surfaced when a heinous crime confronted them. Other than that, he took most everything in stride.

As the boss, Ralph had to dress for the job now. Prior to his promotion, he usually affected a more relaxed style of fashion less clothing, leaning more towards tieless shirts and wrinkled chino slacks. The new and more sophisticated Ralph was more, to his mind only, claustrophobically dressed in three-piece suits, subdued bland ties of no particular design, and scuffed well-worn brogans.

It took the promotion that he did not seek nor want to be the top dog in the Homicide Division to affect this radical change. And, in Ralph's mind, it was a rather large pain in the ass along with a pain in his wallet. Still, he went along with it, as the Chief of Detectives had more or less demanded it when he gave him the promotion to Detective Lieutenant.

Be that as it may, it made no change in Ralph's devotion to the job. He had been courted by an FBI's rather attractive agent several months ago but remained loyal to the N.Y.P.D. where he believed he was needed more. He had thought about the lure of a relationship with Agent Gina Grant and was flattered by her attention and the possibility of a long term and a possible relationship with her, but had made his decision to remain in New York and his job.

Detective Alan Beckman remained the same man he had been for all the years in the department. His only deviation was to seek out a former witness and to agree with her to seriously date on a regular basis, otherwise he remained Ralph's partner and backup second in command.

Chapter Four

In the small town of Arthur, New York, nothing would have surprised them more than the bizarre events that had been reported to their unit. In the last few weeks, reports of individuals having been found in strange situations in South Park, specifically, the northern portion that several biker gangs claimed as their territory.

On two successive mornings, the sector patrolmen reported finding two to three unsavory types, actual gang members, tied to trees, beaten and unconscious, with cryptic notes pinned to their colors. The notes have been included in the incident reports, DD5s, and forwarded to the division.

The town of Arthur is on the outskirts of New York City. Thus, the mayor of Author called the mayor of the city and requested help from the NYPD.

Although no homicides had been reported, the chief thought that the incidents were strange and mysterious enough and at the request of the mayor of Arthur, to call in Ralph and his team to give it their special attention. He decided to give the team a shot at the case.

Ralph would not have given them a second thought but for the insistence of the chief. He had found that the notes left at the scene, most probably by the perp, were in themselves an indication that the author was (1) a very strong individual, (2) a very intelligent and well-read person, and (3) a semi-violent one, given the size and type of victim found tied to the trees.

Given these points, the chief found himself confused. He knew these victims rarely, if ever, traveled solo and that the crews of these guys seldom gave up their territories willingly, so in his mind the perpetrator had to have help. This kind of help required more than two or three others equal to the victim's stature. It seemed inconceivable that only one person could inflict the damage and the ability to take the time and trouble to actually tie one or more of these gang members to the trees and then take even more time to compose a note to accompany them.

Ralph and Alan approached the chief's office and knocked on the frame of his door. "Chief, you wanted to see us?"

"Yes, Ralph, Alan." he greeted them with a dour look on his face "Come in, there's something I want to run past you."

He slid three folders with the tree reports across the desk.

Ralph put his hand out to stop the folders before they slipped off the desk. The Chief said, "I'll wait".

Ralph read the first one and passed it over to Alan who put on his new glasses and gave it his fullest attention. Requests by the Chief of Detectives called for his best effort, as these requests did not come often or taken lightly.

After a few minutes, when all the reports had been scanned, Ralph looked up to the Chief and said, "Very odd and very interesting. But, Chief, why us? There's been no homicide here. It seems as though they have a vigilante working the South Park area."

"I agree," the Chief said "But how long can it be before it does turn into a killing, either the vigilante's or a gang member?"

Chapter Five

When Lew was a child he had experienced these strange phenomenon, but as a young boy, he did not think it was any more than a bad dream. His dreams were somewhat vivid and, sometimes when he woke up, he was drenched in sweat and extremely tired. He wondered what it was that made him this way.

At age ten, he woke up one morning covered with feathers and sweating profusely.

"What is this?" he muttered brushing feathers from his hair and face. Nothing he could do could make him remember the prior night. Try as he might it remained a complete blank to him.

He went to school as if nothing had happened with the exception of his awakenings.

All through the school, the teachers and his classmates were talking about how a coyote or a large wolf had invaded the pen of someone's herd of sheep and chickens. The word going around was that someone or something had fought the animal and prevented it from killing or making off with any of the livestock. Blood was supposed to have been found everywhere at the scene, but none of it appeared to be human.

Lew listened to all the talk and merely went about his school business. He made no comments to anyone, but somewhere deep inside felt an inner satisfaction. He did not know why he felt this way but it was still satisfying.

In the years that went by, he experienced this feeling many times. He was still unaware of what had occurred and how people associated him with these strange happenings.

His mother and father were never aware of anything odd in their only son. They loved him unconditionally and had the greatest hopes for his future. They knew him to be a boy with many friends and people who met him looked upon him as a polite and well-mannered young man.

They had set aside money for his education, which included enough for him to go to college and to concentrate on his studies without the concern of having to work outside of school.

He did have many friends, but not one that he considered his best friend.

There were those who, when he was a teenager, noticed something in him that set him apart from the usual crowd but could never put a finger on what it was.

Then there were those, who even though they seemed to admire him, were a bit suspicious of his absences from school.

Marty Samms considered him his best friend, although Lew was not aware of this.

Marty was a rather chubby boy who had been the butt of many jokes from a lot of the boys and a number of girls. He really could not help the fact that he was heavier and less well dressed than the average kid in school was, but then again he really did not try very hard to trim himself down.

Marty was less concerned about his clothes and even less concerned about his personal cleanliness. So much so that in class other kids would move as far away from his desk as they possibly could, but Marty hardly noticed.

Lew, on the other hand, was fastidious about his own personal cleanliness and his clothing. His hair was always neatly combed. Even after a rigorous gym class, and though haircuts were not so much on his mind, it was always neat.

He liked Marty a lot and tried to look out for him as much as he could whenever the other kids made hurtful comments. Lew would leap to his defense and try to explain Marty's problems.

As far as Lew was concerned, two different classes of people made up the world. There were the ones who could understand and sympathize and the others who were constantly mean, nasty individuals who only wanted to hurt and belittle others to make themselves feel bigger and better about themselves and make the butt of their jokes feel belittled.

Marty was not the only kid in school that had been ostracized and Lew did his best to try to protect every single one of them, but he lacked the skills and could only do so much. It frustrated him, but still he tried.

Chapter Six

The town of Arthur, New York, was situated 15 miles north of the island of Manhattan but was still in its jurisdiction.

The town's population was counted as 25,000 citizens. It was serviced by a main street that contained one attorney's office, one police station with a police chief and five police officers, one real estate office with agents, two beauty shops, one barber shop, one Winn Dixie Supermarket, two drug stores, one large sporting goods store with ten employees, two shoe stores, one Ben & Jerry's ice cream store, one dry goods store, and one accounting office, all of which were in the nicer part of town.

Housed in what would be classified as the bad part of town, were two bars and strip clubs,

one attorney's office, one grocery store, and two
burnt out store buildings in which biker gangs set
up shop and used as hangouts for their rather
ugly businesses.

Surrounding the town was well-to-do
houses, middle class houses, some lower class
houses, and a small mobile home park.

And, lastly 'THE PARK.'

Chapter Seven

Somewhere deep in his memory, and it was very
deep, Lew registered the fact that he had
encountered this type of fog before. It nagged at
the base of his skull, but he had difficulty
bringing it forward to a conscious level. The fog
made it practically impossible for logical
thoughts to form. He could only go with the flow
of it and so as he moved as if in a dream.

However, this dream fog seemed so
different, a dark foreboding was tugging at the
base of his brain, and it was not a good feeling.
He tried to think it away, but there never was any
room for thought, only the dense fog.

It lasted the entire night and in the
morning, with the sunlight filtering through the
blinds in his bedroom, he awoke, not refreshed
by a night of supposedly restful sleep, but totally
exhausted as if he had toiled the entire night. His

bedclothes were still draped across the end of the bed and as he looked down, the clothes that he was wearing were soiled and reeking of some kind of greasy smell. They were stained with an unrecognizable type of brown pigment.

His hair was a tangled mess and there was something, a sticky something, which was quite foreign to him. Since he was always so well groomed and pristinely clean, he felt nauseous at the sights and smells associated with him at the moment as he pushed himself up and staggered to his bathroom.

The sight that greeted him in the bathroom mirror frightened him. In addition to the state of his clothing and hair, his face had stains of dirt and several scratches, like someone had raked their fingernails down the side of his face and had drawn blood.

A sickening feeling came over Lew. He had no idea what he had done the night before in the fog, but it was dawning on him that whatever it was it was not good.

In the meantime, his wife Linda had arisen long before he came home and had left for her job. She was quite used to waking up and not finding him in the bed.

He had somehow managed to drag himself home without anyone seeing him and he was glad of that fact.

Chapter Eight

What Lew had not remembered, and what all of his neighbors did remember and lauded him for had happened that night in December.

Lew was in one of his deepest fogs when he happened to come upon a group of bikers that had encircled two of the neighborhood's teenaged girls. Girls who were of high school age and were not wise yet in the ways of life and grown up boys, actually, these were men… of sorts.

Bobby Perlak, or as he was known in biker circles as Bobby Pearl, was the titular leader of this grisly crew of seven. He sported a triple strand of white pearls around his rather filthy neck and wore a rag tag assortment of leather and jeans with scuffed boots of a color that had been originally black, but now were a torn and filthy brown.

His close buddy, Bernie Campon, known by the crude name Bernie Tampon, and six other unsavory bikers surrounded the two naïve teenagers.

They were pushing the young targets around in a circle. Rough hands grabbing and touching these young girls wherever they could touch. The girls naturally were terrified. As well they should have been, because these characters meant very nasty business.

Lew was walking blindly into the midst of this mess. He saw, but did not take into account, that he was outnumbered eight to one. However, in his state, he gave it no credence.

As soon as he was touched and touched rather roughly, his eyes took on an eerie glow.

He whirled around and faced Bobby Pearl, who immediately smiled thinking, "Oh boy, more fun".

Lew also smiled, which took the Pearl by surprise since what he saw was a man about 5'10" weighing about 175 lbs. compared to Pearl's 6'3" 225 lb. muscular frame.

"Child's play," Pearl said through a sideways-mouthed comment to his motley friends.

"You betta back off man," a biker said, standing to one side, as Lew approached the Pearl "I really don't like your chances, little man".

Bobby Pearl stood up to his full height and glared at Lew.

A low growl rumbled from Lew's throat, unlike his normal voice that was soft and never threatening.

"Take my advice and move on. You don't want to tangle with me."

Bobby Pearl broke out in raucous laughter, "Did you hear what this pipsqueak said to me?" he turned to his gang of creeps, "Ha, ha, ha,"

He turned back to Lew, "I gave you a chance to run, but now, it's too late".

Again, that deep rumble emanated from Lew's throat, "Pal, you may laugh now, but the laugh will be on you. I guarantee it."

While this was happening, the two girls took their chance and quietly slipped away. They started running as soon as they felt it was safe to do so.

They ran and ran, not speaking but breathing sighs of relief at being away from the danger they had been facing moments before.

When they stopped running and caught their breath, they looked at each other and agreed they had been lucky. "But what about the little man? Should we call the cops?" The question died in their throats and they decided to just go home and try to forget the whole incident.

Chapter Nine

The absence of the two girls went unnoticed, all the attention of the bikers was concentrated on the little man that stood before them, defiantly questioning their right to harass and if it came to it, physically do harm to whomever they deemed they had every right to do.

"You don't know who you are dealing with, do you?" Bobby asked, as he pressed closer to Lew's face, spittle forming on the corners of his ugly scarred mouth. "I've &#!+ bigger things than you on a bad day. So why don't you turn your little tail around and get the hell out of my face?"

Deep in his mind, Lew noted that this ugly bozo spoke harshly, but had a twinge of fear in his voice. In his fog state he didn't rationalize his decision, and that this man, this ragged leathered person before him, this weak draped half excuse of a man, was deep down afraid of not only him, but afraid of looking like he could be scared of anything or anyone.

Lew pressed on, and it appeared, that in his own mind, he could and should show this dressed up clown just who was the better man.

"Okay," he grumbled softly, "I think you have bothered enough people who probably thought that you were someone to be feared and that they were the ones that owed you something, that if you wanted to you could force them to do it. But, the time has come to call a halt to your intimidation of the weaker ones. I don't fear you because you're actually the weak one who has no self-worth. You think that because you are bigger and scarier looking, that you can continue your so-called domination of others, that you can be a bully. Well, that ends here and now. DO YOU UNDERSTAND ME?"

Bobby just stepped back with a look on his face that defied understanding by his friends, who also looked at Lew with something akin to awe written on their faces. Faces, which on some of them had weird facial hair that looked like they had not shaved or washed in months.

Bobby stammered, "What, what did you just say to me? I don't understand. Do ya mean that you're not scared of me? Do ya mean that I'm afraid of a little squirt like you? HA, I think you got the wrong guy here. What do you know about me and what I am?"

"I know that you don't want to look weak in front of your buddies. But, look at them. Look at their faces. They know whom and what you are, and you really know what you are. You pose and threaten, but you don't really believe that you are the fierce animal that you want your friends here to think. That deep down inside, despite your size, you're just a little man who was probably abused by your parents when you were young. Do I have that right? I do, don't I?" Lew said.

"I, uh, um," Bobby stuttered, "I don't know what you're talking about."

"Oh, sure you do. Think man. Think about when you were younger. If you remember, you can come to grips with your real self. You don't have to do this. You can ride your motorcycle and all that, but you don't have to put on this act.

Look at your friends. Do you think they respect you? No, they don't. They have their own issues they have to deal with. They know, and they are thinking about themselves and their upbringing. They only hang out with you because of the mob mentality. One on one, they are just as insecure as you are. They now realize that, and that I am right. So…what do you want to do now?"

In a last ditch effort to bolster himself, Bobby, who had just been reduced by Lew's words, blurted out, "You think you know everything do you? Well, you don't. I'm bigger and tougher than you, and I can snuff you anytime I want."

He looked at his gang members with an oily smirk on his face, winking at them, attempting to regain their support.

They all looked at him for an instant and then all eyes looked down and inspected the pavement with a great deal of interest.

"Guy's, what do you think? Should I snuff this little man now, or what?"

His little band of motley bikers turned their backs on him and stumbled away, leaving him alone with Lew, who stood his ground and gazed intently at him.

"Look", Bobby said, in a distinctly different voice, "I don't want to hurt you, I just wanted to scare you and those girls. I'm not as bad as you think. Why don't we just go about our own business and forget about this, okay?"

"Well, you know that I'm going to be around, and that even though I think you might change your ways, I'm going to be watching you. And, if it happens that I think you are responsible for anything, and I don't care what, I'll be back for you. Do we understand each other?"

"Yeah, yeah, I understand", he said and did a quick about face and rushed away.

Chapter Ten

"Chief, I still don't see a reason, except that you want Alan and I on this supposed case. There doesn't seem to be a crime here, much less a homicide," Ralph said in all earnestness.

"Ralph, I know what you're saying and I agree with you, but the mayor has made a request and somehow I just can't ignore such a request coming from him personally, now can I?"

"But Chief, we have other more pressing cases that need to be investigated, how about the double murder in the Soho district, and the killing of that little boy in Harlem, not to mention all the other cases that the squad is working on that are more important than a vigilante who hasn't hurt or killed anyone."

"I know, I know, and I agree with you Ralph, but it's the mayor."

"And, I reiterate, Chief. It's not homicide's type of case. Why don't you give it to Victims Division? It's right up their alley."

"Don't you get it detective? I'm the chief and you're the detective, and now I'm giving you the order. This is your case and I expect you to do the job I'm assigning you. Have you got that now?" the Chief said, with a hint of irritation in his voice.

"Yes sir, Chief. I got it and thanks for your confidence," Ralph said with further hint of condescension in his voice.

"There's no reason for us to be acting like this, Ralph. You and I know this isn't a perfect world. We both have to do some things we really don't want to do. But look at it this way; so far there are no bodies to process…yet."

"Okay, Chief. Of course you are right", Ralph softened and saluted while he backed away out of his office, thinking, "The man has a hard enough job to do, why should I make it any harder?"

He thought as he walked back to his squad, "How am I going to break this to the guys? They'll never believe it, but then, neither do I."

Chapter Eleven

Lew watched him go and had a satisfying feeling in his heart and mind, that he had done something so profoundly good, but almost immediately, he could not remember exactly what had happened.

He looked around, he could not remember how or where he was, the fog was still around him and seemed to deepen as he looked behind and all around. Where was he? Although he recognized that, he was in sort of a park, with trees and grass, but it did not come to his mind just then.

Turning, he began to walk. There was no definite direction that he had decided upon, he just walked.

After a time, and he felt it had to have been a long time for it was coming on to dawn, light started to filter through the fog and he began to see sights, houses, and street signs that he recognized.

Somehow or other he was returning home.

"My, my, I must have taken some walk this morning. Linda must have breakfast ready. I'd better get home."

Chapter Twelve

As Bobby Pearl revved up his tricked out Harley and roared away, he began to think, he wondered about what had just happened. Here was this little guy standing up to him and his seven biker friends. He couldn't believe that this little twerp had taken the play away from him, he had stood up to him and let those two ripe, luscious teeny boppers get away from him, "Damn," he had talked him out of dealing with him the way he had always dealt with guys that got in his face.

Prior to this encounter, he had meted out punishment for even the most trivial of reasons, there did not have to be a big deal involved in any of his former fights, he just took control and did whatever came to his mind.

However, this, this incident was really strange and it confused him to no end.

"How could this happen?" he asked himself amid the roar of his and two of his cohorts.

The same thing was going through Bernie Tampon's mind as they raced down the highway, heading for their favorite biker bar.

"Man, Bobby was in control of everything until that little guy showed up and then...and then...he didn't. The little guy stepped right up to him and faced him down...with...something!!!"

What he did not know, but it was …something, something that came off the guy, like, it was strange and he felt it too, but not as much as apparently Bobby did.

Bernie Tampon was 30 years old and had been a biker a good ten of those years. He had seen all kinds of weird things in those years, riding with all types. Bobby Pearl was one of the meanest he had ridden with, bar none. He was a big man, with muscles rippling from under his leathers and was not shy about showing and telling just how tough he was. And, man, he was tough, until…tonight.

He had never seen this side of Bobby. The man just evaporated. His toughness disappeared, and he looked just like any other wannabe biker, all brag, and no-nothing.

"I'm no patsy myself and I felt a power from this guy that was like none other I have gotten from anyone," he thought to himself.

"I better stop thinking like this. Bobby and the other fellas must be able to see us like this, and that ain't good."

Bobby Pearl was also thinking the same thoughts, "How am I going to look in front of these other guys. I hope no one tells about this. I got to get my head back on straight or they'll see it on my face."

The worry about how he looked to his friends was making his face contort. Luckily, he had a visor that covered his face and Bernie could not see him, and he maintained a steady speed that kept him well in front of them.

Still, his mind kept coming back to what had happened, he tried to rationalize it but could not quite wrap his mind around the whole thing.

Chapter Thirteen

The Manhattan District Attorney's office was quiet, eerily quiet. No meetings had been scheduled for the morning, and all the attorneys were in their assigned offices. The phones had been unusually dormant for a Tuesday morning.

It was strange that even the most senior ADAs had no cases pending and the investigators for the city had not brought in anything worth pursuing. Not that they were responsible for drumming up business for the District Attorney's office, but every once in a while they were tipped off to information about crimes that would be of some concern.

It was ADA Andrew Jackson, whose office overlooked lower Wall Street, and perused the passing parade of men, women, and vehicles was jolted out of his reverie by the insistent buzz of his phone.

He was deep in thought at that moment planning his vacation, which was coming in a few weeks. Thoughts of a cruise were broken by the insistence of the phone.

"ADA Jackson", he intoned as he put the receiver to his ear.

"Sir, you have a Lt. Bloom at the 21st Precinct on the phone, sir," his secretary Shelly Fallon said.

"Okay, put him through."

Shelly Fallon had been Andrews' secretary for his entire time with the DA's office and rarely appeared to be rattled at any of the weird things that came through the doors of the offices.

She was efficient to the nth degree and ran Andy's particular office like a Fortune 500 corporation. She was conscientious to a fault and had adopted Jackson, and although there was no romantic interest between the two, she protected him as she would a lover. No one that she did not like or trust gained entry or an introduction to him without being subjected to her stern inquisitions.

Shell dressed the part, in severe business suits with little or no jewelry adorning her person.

She had been married early and had been much maligned by her former husband of five years, which led to a rather vicious divorce that had soured her towards most men who appeared to want to dominate her. Her short marriage resulted in her giving birth to a son who took after her husband so much that he demanded all of her time from birth to the time that her ex-spouse gained custody by virtue of her time devoted to her career with little or no time left to care for her son.

For her it was a relief, not having to be a mother or wife and concentrating all her time on her boss, herself, and her job providing all the excitement and fulfillment for which she could hope.

Shelly lived in an efficient one bedroom apartment that provided all the amenities she needed, a pool, gym, recreation room for workouts, a meeting room for condominium business, and all the privacy she could ever want or need.

She paid no attention to neighbors and their problems, went in and out of her building with her head down, and went about her business all by herself.

A little wine after her day's work provided all the relaxation she needed to put her to sleep at night, no dreams, no interruptions, with the possible exception of a call to work on rare occasions.

Chapter Fourteen

When Lew returned home, nothing was made of his nights outing. His only son, who had just started talking at the age of two, approached his father and in his childish voice simply said, "Daddy, where were you?"

"Just out son," Lew replied as he bent to his hug his son, "Just out".

Satisfied, the little boy waddled away seemingly happy at that answer, but Lew was not.

"I wonder where I was and what I did," he mused at the back of his son's retreating figure. "I just wonder."

He did not waste any more time wondering, he had to get ready to go to work. Slowly he made his way upstairs to shower and shave. He was not going to waste any more time on last night, and he only knew he had done…something.

Linda went about her daily routine. She picked up his clothes from where he dropped them prior to going into the shower. She went through his pockets, not looking for anything important, but to remove his wallet and whatever change he might have accumulated during the day.

She did this every day with no surprises in his belongings. Only this morning, as she put her hand deep down in his right front pocket, her hand touched a strange foreign object. As she withdrew the object, she looked down at a semi-large, spring-loaded switchblade, looking like it had seen more than one usage.

She dropped it on the top of Lew's nightstand and just stared at it as if it were an alien being, and to her it was.

"What the," she started to say aloud to herself when Lew stepped into the room. He looked up to see Linda staring down at an object on the nightstand.

"Lynn, what's wrong?" he was concerned by the look on her face.

"Lew, what is this, I know it's a knife, but where did you get it? Is it yours? Why do you have it?"

"Whoa, one question at a time let me see what you have there, Oh my gawd, where did that come from?" he exclaimed loudly, "That's not mine. Where did it come from? What are you doing with it?"

Linda met this explosion of questions with a repeat of her own questions, "Whoa there, Lew. I asked you first. You can't ask me the same questions I ask you. Can you explain how this got into your pocket? "

"No, I can't. I've never seen that thing before."

"Well, it didn't just crawl into your pocket now, did it?"

"No, it probably didn't. But I can't tell you because I don't know."

"Lew, you were out most of the night. Don't you remember where you were and what you did?" as soon as she said this she realized she was asking an impossible question, given his oddly strange comings and goings.

"Ah… again…no."

Linda added, "This had better not be about anything like someone getting hurt with this", as she picked up the knife between her first two fingers, handling it very gingerly, and pushing it towards Lew.

"Don't give to me, I'm telling you I don't know anything about that thing. I've never seen it before and I don't want to see it anymore," he said, shrinking away from the approaching object in his wife's hand.

"Lew, we've got to give it to the police. It may be that it was used and they might want to check it out. Take it and put it in something and give it to them."

"Should I take it or should I just forget about it?" he asked being perfectly serious.

Speaking in a voice that he recognized as her being adamant she said, "Take it, Lew!"

Chapter Fifteen

Bobby Pearl and his cronies revved up their
motorcycles, creating a crescendo of noise that
completely shut out any conversation and or
traffic sound that usually accompanied the daily
life on the street.

Again and again, they revved up their
bikes, and anyone who dared to complain or even
looked askance at them would incur either
outward violence or harassment in one form or
another.

The plan was to ride into the park, make
their presence known, and possibly find either a
female escorted or not and failing that, some
older person or persons who in their innocence
were only looking for some peace and quiet that
the park was supposed to offer.

After patrolling the park and finding no
one of even minor importance, the gang retreated
to their current clubhouse, an abandoned store on
a side street in the downtown district.

Bobby plopped himself down on a three-
legged discarded lounge chair, propped up by a
soda crate to make it more stable. The leatherette,
that was once shiny and studded by brass nail
heads, was torn and faded to a threadbare grey
and no one but Bobby was allowed to sit on it. To
do so would be reason for Bobby to haul that
someone up and beat him, with no mercy, until

bruised and bloody. Up until the other night, this was his hold on the gang, complete and utter subservience by the gang, but that had noticeably changed.

"Boys," Bobby announced to the group, that consisted of some older members who had given up the title of 'BOYS' to the newest members that barely had started to grow some fuzz on their pale faces. "I promise you some action tonight. We're either going to find a likely subject in the park or, if we don't, I have a plan for us to make a big score. I leave it up to you. Which one would youse guys prefer?"

The majority took no big thrill in harassing the old and infirm, though a ripe female or two usually would satisfy their lust hailed, "Big score, big score", loudly.

"Okay, but you got to listen and do what I say, nobody does nuthin' I don't tell him to do, get it?" Bobby yelled above the noise.

"Right, Bobby. Anything you say", Bernie Tampon said and held his hands up for quiet.

The gang took a few minutes to quiet down and give Bobby their full attention, some mumbling could be heard, but basically, he had their attention.

"Okay, you know that sporting goods store over on Fifth? The one that carries everything. Well, I know for a fact that they put together their payroll tomorrow and they only have one person as security. We hit them just before closing. There should be no customers at that time, but if there are, we take what they got, too. What I need is one or two of you in the store around 6:00 to act as lookouts and let me know if the coast is clear. Who wants to volunteer for lookout?"

Several hands went up and Bobby told Bernie to take them aside and tell them what he wanted them to do and where to be located in the store.

"We are only going to need five of you on this job. Of course, we divvy up the loot with all of you but too many will be, like, too obvious. So, Bernie will choose who's going along. Okay, see Bernie."

"Anyone who thinks he can do this come to over to the big table and we'll talk it over," Bernie called out, and immediately the entire gang filed over to the table.

"Hold it. I only need three guys and two lookouts, so some of you chill out. I know we all want to be in, but I can't use you all."

Slowly the crowd around the table thinned out and Bernie made his choices.

Duanne, an older biker with a large handlebar moustache and huge flowing red beard, was choice number one. He wore the traditional biker leathers, jacket, jeans, boots, and was baldheaded under his helmet.

Carl, also an older biker, whose face was devoid of facial hair, sported a long ponytail. He wore denims, and the boots were a fake cowboy style that did not come up over his ankles and had side zippers.

Those two were going to go in with Bobby and Bernie. The two lookouts were young members who were more or less cleaner looking and would be more acceptable as customers in a sporting goods store and not stand out as bikers.

They would wear a more normal, civilian type of outfit that would blend in with the stores concept.

Bobby and Bernie conducted detailed plans for the assault and after a few hours broke for the night to mull over their plans.

Chapter Sixteen

Blood was everywhere, it covered the glass on the doors and the front checkout counters, it covered the front racks of team shirts that had been turned over, indicating the obvious frantic scrambling of bodies trying to get out of the store.

Deeper into the body of the stores depth, a mound of clothes and sports equipment hid a form that would later be discovered by the first responders on the scene as a dead body.

The call went out at 4:10 a.m. when the silent alarm sounded at the security company. No one knew why it had taken so long for the alarm to be activated, but at the time, no one cared.

A sector car was dispatched to the location. Upon its arrival, they observed the iron security gate pulled away from its moorings. It would be determined later that a car or truck had been hooked up to the gate and yanked it out forcibly, leaving the glass doors vulnerable to being cut open by a glasscutter.

It took ten minutes for the sector car to respond, as it was more than five miles away on the other side of its district.

Immediately upon their arrival, they called for backup and waited outside the store before entering.

So, in essence, it was 20 minutes more before entry was accomplished!

Patrolman Sam Urban stepped carefully around the blood spatters that greeted him upon entry. He shined his flashlight around and observed the chaos of the entryway.

"Sarge," he whispered to the second responder and the senior officer to arrive, "Do you think anyone's still in here?"

"I wouldn't take it for granted that they have left, but I don't think there's anyone alive in there either," Sgt Kelly said quietly.

"I'll go left, Sarge. Okay?"

"Okay. I'll get Simmons to flank the right side. I'll go down the center aisle."

Officer Nicholas Bell, a third patrolman, walked behind Kelly and swept the center aisle with his light. They walked stealthily, their eyes swinging back and forth, looking and alert for any movement, sensing danger at every open space.

"Sarge, look", Bell pointed to the mound off to the side of the aisle. "What do you think that could be?" he also whispered as if there was someone who could overhear him.

"Don't touch anything, we'll let CSU (Crime Scene Unit) get it untangled, just keep your eyes open and stay alert."

"Roger, Sarge."

"Urban," Kelly called out, "Have you found anything yet?"

"No, Sarge. Nothing but a lot of mess over here."

"Simmons, how about you? Have you got anything to report?"

"Sarge, there's a lot of damage over here. It looks like they were trying to get the outboard motors and the rifle and gun cabinet are open. It looks like it was almost jimmied open but nothing's missing, so far as I can see."

"Okay, don't touch anything. Let the crime scene guys do their jobs. Let's just secure the scene and wait for them. I already called it in. Check the rear exit and I'll be right there."

"Got it, Sarge," Patrolman Simmons said.

Chapter Seventeen

Something was happening to Lew, something that had begun to dawn on him. It was not his late night outings or the awakenings that had confused and worried him. It was the reactions of the people he met at the store and on the street. The open adoration that they showed at seeing him totally threw him.

That morning he arrived at the Triangle Sports Shops where he worked as the assistant manager at his usual 9:10 a.m. The store's personnel were already there and at his arrival, all the workers gathered around him and broke into instant applause, with cheers and slaps on his back. He of course had no idea what prompted this outbreak, but he took it in his usual non-committal way, and proceeded to his office. The office was the way it always was. He was surrounded by goods that still had to be assessed as to their ability to draw good sales outcome.

He wondered what he had done to merit all the adoration, when his desk phone jingled indicating that the manager wanted him to produce himself in his office.

Again he wondered, he did a lot of wondering lately and he was wondering again... again the wondering why the early call to the manager's office.

"Oh, well," he thought, "Might as well see what he has on his mind this morning," and he set out across to the other side of the store.

"Hi, Mr. Martin. How are you this morning?"

"Lew, you've been here for years, longer than I, and how many times have I asked you to call me Bob? That's my name, you know. So, you kind of don't have to call me Mr. Martin or sir. Can you find in your heart to do that? After all we are friends, aren't we?"

"Yes, sir. I mean, Bob. It's just the way I have been brought up, polite. You know?"

"Okay, but I don't think this is the last time I'm going to have this conversation. Anyway, Lew, what have you been up to? I mean what happened now?"

"Bob, to tell you the truth...I don't know."

"You don't know? All the help know, I obviously don't know or I wouldn't be asking. Maybe we should ask someone out there on the floor what you've done."

"I don't know," Lew's head was spinning, "I don't know if I really want to find out, maybe... maybe I did something wrong."

"Well, I don't think that's the case. If you did something wrong they wouldn't have reacted the way they did when you walked in, would they?"

"I don't know what to say sir...er...Bob."

"Don't say anything, Lew. Just keep doing what you're doing and as far as your job, great job Lew," Bob Martin said as he held out his hand and shook Lew's warmly.

"Thanks, Bob," Lew said walking back to his office in a cloud of confusion.

"I just hope, whatever I've done won't come back to bite me," he mused to himself.

Chapter Eighteen

"Really, Chief, I don't see that there's a crime here" Ralph said.

"We've gotten only rumors about someone. We have no eyewitnesses, reports of foul play, just stories that this person steps in at certain times and prevents things from happening. Truthfully, all I see is a Good Samaritan being there when he or she is needed. That's good for us...isn't it?"

"Ralph, I agree with you, but I have had a report that a biker was stabbed the night before last. He is in the hospital, and they don't know if he will make it. If he doesn't then we have a potential vigilante killer out there. I don't know if it's the same person, but it needs looking into. It's not a homicide, yet. But, it could become one. Let's just take Alan and check it out."

"Okay, Chief" Ralph said.

Ralph left the chief's office and casually chatted with the other cops before going back to his precinct to inform Alan about their new assignment. He felt a little embarrassed at getting a nuisance assignment from the Chief of Detectives but as he always said to himself and others, "You get a job; you do it the best you can."

As he got back to his office, he paged his partner, "Alan, please come to my office for a minute, would you?"

He felt a little foolish, they had enough legitimate crimes to concern themselves with at the time, but…well…the Chief…

"You rang, my friend?" Alan said with a smile as he passed through Ralph's open door.

"Why, of course I did. Didn't you get the memo? When I ring, everything goes on hold until I'm satisfied. I wrote the memo myself, but, almost seriously, I have the Chief of D's request to comply with and he made it especially clear that he wanted you on the case."

"Me, a case, a triple murder, or an assault on the mayor, something I can sink my teeth into?" he asked a little bit tongue-in-cheek wise.

"No, Alan. Not quite," Ralph said as he went on to fill Alan in about the case the chief had handed them.

"I need you to go over to Arthur Hospital. Take one of the troops with you, preferably one of the new ones, and get the lowdown from this biker Bobby Perlak. Get his story and follow up on whatever needs following up."

"Ralph, is this a joke the chief's playing on us? Does he really believe there's a case for us in this? I mean, compared to what we have on the table, this is a little, may I say it?… Stupid."

"Al, I know exactly what this is, but a request from the chief and also the mayor is really, and you know it…an order plain and simple. So, we do what he requests. And, maybe we can get in a little R&R for ourselves out of it. Lawd knows we need it. So get your butt to the hospital, okay?"

"I guess", Alan said and left to go choose his sidekick for the job.

"Charlie," Alan called out, "I need you.

Charlene Soldana, a rather robust Hispanic woman of about 30 stood up, adjusted her clothes, and crossed the room to Alan's desk.

Charlene wore a black pantsuit with a grey man-tailored blouse under the jacket, which housed a shoulder holster that was not exactly invisible, especially when the jacket was unbuttoned. She wore unfashionable black shoes that did not add to her femininity, but were useful to a detective on the job.

"What can I do for you, Detective Beckman?" she asked with a little lilt to her voice. She thought Alan was a little sweet on her. To tell the truth she was not quite Alan's type, but he kept a cheerful tone to his approach.

"Charlie, we've got a little job to do. Grab your notebook and call down for a unit. We have to go to a hospital to interview someone."

"Right, Detective. I'm on it," she said and picked up the phone to order a car.

Chapter Nineteen

Lulu Benson and Sylvia Warren sat at an industrial-type green desk covered with an eight-year-old desk calendar with numerous phone numbers and doodles scribbled across its face.

A uniformed police officer sat across from them with a halfway interested face looking back at their obviously nervous ones.

Lulu was 16 years old, as was her girlfriend Sylvia. They looked at each other, doubts written across their young faces.

Lulu was dressed in the latest jeans, with built in rips and tears across the thighs and knees and had a hooded sweatshirt of vibrant blue over a white tee shirt. Her hair was fashionably tipped blond on blond and tied in the back.

Sylvia was more conservatively dressed in black denim slacks and a white man-tailored shirt, her hair was short and neatly combed back.

"Okay, girls," the officer said stonily, "Tell me what you think you saw two nights ago?"

Lulu was first to speak, "Sir, it's not what we think we saw, we were there."

"Yes," Sylvia spoke up, "We were approached by a biker gang in the park."

"Central Park, right?"

"Right, we were walking home on the Morningside Path."

"Yes," Sylvia cried, "All of a sudden we were surrounded by these guys. I think. No; I know they meant to rape us or more."

"Wait a minute." Officer Raymond Tornillo said, "You're sure they were out to rape you girls?"

Lulu looked at him as if he was either stupid or really naïve, "Look officer, I know you can't think like a girl. But, we know hands down when someone, especially a biker, looks at us like he wants to be more than a pen pal. You get what I mean, sir?"

"Sir," Sylvia interjected, "Haven't you ever looked at a girl or a woman, and said to yourself, 'I would like to be more than friends with her?'"

"Er, uh, I don't think what I think or don't is germane to this complaint you're making against these guys. Let's continue, okay?"

"Right, the thing is, when it was getting heavy, this little guy comes out of the dark and faces the bikers down. I mean, he walked right up to the biggest guy and stood between him and us," Lulu said.

"And who is this guy?" Officer Raymond asked.

"We don't know, he just told us to leave and then he talked to the biker. We left, but stopped a little ways away to see what would happen. You know if maybe the guy might have gotten hurt, there were at least six bikers against him. You know what I'm saying?"

"I get it young lady, so what did happen?"

"Well," Sylvia piped up, "They talked for about five minutes, and all of a sudden the big biker just turns away and takes his friends with him. The little guy just stands there watching them leave."

"They just left?"

"Yes, and then the little guy turned around and disappeared into the park."

"So what do you want us to do about this?"

"Well, we just want you, the police, to be aware that these guys are out there in the park and looking to cause trouble, and maybe you can put someone out there at night. I mean, you might even want to find this little guy, he's a hero, to us anyway," Lulu said, with Sylvia shaking her head in agreement.

"Okay, I'm certainly going to submit your request upstairs. It's up to them what they'll do."

"Thank you sir, we appreciate you taking the time and we hope you can find our hero."

"You're quite welcome ladies, and we will definitely look into it. Thanks for coming in."

Chapter Twenty

Linda Wallace looked at the knife as it lay on the counter top. She could not understand anything about its strange appearance and much more, she could not understand anything about her husband's comings and goings, especially lately.

She desperately wanted to ask him about his sojourns, but he did not seem to understand them himself.

He came out of the shower and walked into the kitchen where Linda was still standing looking down at the offending object.

With his robe hanging on his spare frame and a dejected look on his face, he put his arms around her from the back and kissed the back of her neck softly.

"Are you alright, Hon?"

"No," she said, "This bothers me more than a lot. I have so many questions."

"I know," Lew said. "So do I, but I don't have any answers. Really, it's a mystery to me too."

"But, Lew, you're such a good man, the best I ever knew. How can whatever-this-is happen?"

"Lynn, I know. The only thing I remember is that I seem to go into some sort of fog and when it happens, everything is a blank. I then find myself in a place that's completely foreign to me. You know, this isn't such a big town but I would never even think of going into some of the places I find myself in."

"I don't think I've ever hurt anyone. I don't think that's in me, but," he hesitated for about sixty seconds, and then shook his head "How can I be sure?"

Lew Wallace was such a good man, so solid a husband and father. It was inconceivable that he could do anything that could be looked upon as wrong. Still, in his mind he was so unsettled he did not know.

"Lew, would you tell me if you remember anything that could be considered bad?" Linda spoke so softly it was difficult for Lew to hear and to respond.

Chapter Twenty-One

At the Arthur Hospital, a man in biker leathers staggered into the emergency room entrance. He was bleeding profusely and as he approached the nurse's station, he fell forwards, his hand clutching his crotch, where the stain of fresh blood soiled his leather pants.

"Code Red, at ER", pealed over the loudspeakers, as the lone nurse rushed around her station.

"Holy &#!+," she said, "Someone cut this guy's dick off!!!"

"Anybody got a clamp, we've got to stop this bleeding", a second nurse dropped to her knees to place compressors over the wound.

A team of nurses and an intern showed up almost immediately and went to work.

"Get him on a gurney, and let's get him into a room. Get an IV of D5W started and a transfusion as soon as we get his blood type."

"What a mess," Nurse Elba Mellon said," Someone's really done a number on this one".

"We'll be lucky to stabilize him, he's lost a lot of blood," the ER intern said.

"I'll call the authorities," Nurse Ava Jackson said as she went to the front desk.

The man on the gurney moaned as his eyes fluttered open. He barely got out "Oh man, it hurts", before he lapsed into unconsciousness again.

Nurse Mellon said, "I'll bet."

"Okay, he's B negative. Let's get a couple of bags over here," the doctor said. "Maybe we can save this one, although I doubt if he's one of the good ones. Let's get cracking, people."

"Yes, Doctor", they all said in unison.

They started cutting away his pants and observed his filthy underwear, that hadn't seen soap or water for a long, long time.

"Ugh," Nurse Mellon said, "This one doesn't believe in personal cleanliness. I'm sure he understands the concept of hygiene. But again, maybe not." she thought to herself.

"I've seen cleaner clothes on the homeless. This is definitely not an upstanding citizen."

At that moment two sector patrolmen entered the room, they stood to one side as the doctor peeled off his sterile gloves and motioned them outside the room.

"I'm Dr. La Polla," he nodded to the patrolmen. "That guy in there got his penis cut off with what appears to be a double bladed knife, but that's up to crime scene guys to determine. That's my estimation. He's very critical because of loss of blood, which we are presently pumping into him. His pants are over there," he pointed to the bloody mess on the floor of the room, "Maybe he has ID in a wallet in there."

"Okay, Doc. We'll check it out. What do you think his chances are? I mean do you think, ah, never mind. It's not your job to determine homicides or not," the patrolman said.

"Swell," the doctor said, "Now let me get back to my patient before you guys ask me to solve your crime for you. Maybe after we get him stable he will be able to help you out."

"You're right, Doc. We'll let you get on with your job. We'll have to wait, but we'll be right over there. Let us know if he comes around," he said as he pointed to two chairs by the entrance to the ER.

"While we're waiting we better call this one in" the patrolman said.

Chapter Twenty-Two

Ralph and Alan drove the short distance to the town of Arthur in relative silence. Alan's mind drifted in and out thinking about how long they would be relegated to this small town with it's out of proportion problem. The scenery changed from the skyscrapers of the big city to fields with cows and an occasional horse making an appearance. Crops of things that were foreign to him sprouted up from virtually nowhere. Homes separated by acres of farmlands passed by and looked so lonely and forlorn that Alan could not fathom living in such seclusion, he seemed to need the activity of a bustling city.

Ralph, on the other hand was off in his own thoughts, driving at a comfortable 45 mph. He envied the quietude of the passing scene.

"Man, what I wouldn't give to live in a nice quiet place like this", He mused to himself. "No sirens in the middle of the night and all day long. No rampant crime or emergencies. I wonder if I will ever see the day if and when I retire, maybe I can handle this type of life."

"Three miles from town, Ralph," Alan interrupted his thoughts "I just saw the sign."

"Yep, I saw it too."

"What do you think we'll find?"

"I think we've got to go to the police chief first, and get the lay of the land, and then we see where we're at with this turkey."

"I think the lay of the land looks great, but very quiet, too quiet for my tastes."

"Yeah, but it has its attractions."

"I don't know, maybe after we're here a while I'll see the attraction, but I still prefer the city."

"Okay, here we are. Now to find the police station."

It took only five minutes to locate the large three-story building, constructed of strong looking red brick with what looked like real marble hosting its entrance. Two heavy oak doors with oversized bronze handles afforded entrance to a large room with a uniformed female officer, seated at a medium sized desk with three phones, and a large ledger facing the doors.

Ralph and Alan approached and flashed their badges. The officer with a nameplate Snyder affixed to the front pocket of her uniform name greeted them with a smile and asked what she could do for them.

"We need to see your chief," Ralph said.

"Okay, please hold on, I'll page him."

Ralph and Alan watched as she pressed a panel on the desk and smiled again at them, "It'll only be a minute, he'll be right with out."

Alan thought as she smiled a smile with gleaming white, evenly spaced teeth, "What a honey. This may not be as bad as I first thought."

Ralph noticed Alan's interest immediately and thought, "Oh my, Alan falls in love so quickly, and I hope he doesn't let it get in the way".

"Snyder, why didn't you let me know these gentlemen were here? We've been waiting for them."

Holding out a large hand, the huge man said, "I'm Chief Lewis, Harvey to you. Welcome to Arthur. Your Chief of Detectives has gracefully let me avail us of your services and expertise and

I, er, we appreciate you coming here and helping."

"Well, Chief, we'll do our best. Why don't we go back to your office and you can fill us in. This is my partner Alan Beckman, and you of course know I'm Detective Bloom, Ralph."

"Good, follow me," he said as he strode off with Alan and Ralph trailing behind him.

Chapter Twenty-Three

While Ralph and the chief were getting acquainted, Alan was wandering around the station. He was a little amazed at the preponderance of electronic equipment that graced every available space. He mused to himself that all the electronics must have cost from $50,000 to 75,000, more than what Ralph and Alan's squad had been allocated at their squad room.

"Alan", Ralph called out. "Are you hearing what the chief here is saying? The situation is more than he or his people are used to and they would appreciate any input from us as we can offer."

"Yes, we can handle the little crime that has been happening, but this recent occurrence has my little force completely baffled. There is no one, and I know most everyone in town, that I can say could or would be responsible for this type of crime."

"Can you offer any hint of anyone that would be capable of this kind of thing, since you know these people?" Ralph asked.

"No, I have almost everyone's profile in the computers and you can access them at your pleasure."

"Okay, Chief. I'm going to get one of our computer techs from the city out here to handle that job. Alan and I are not qualified to utilize computers, except for the basics."

"You can use our guy. But whatever you think is best, you're the detectives", the chief said with no rancor in his voice.

Alan was still wandering around the squad and noticed little or no awards or testimonials hanging on the office walls. He did notice a shadow box with various types of handguns hanging behind the Chief's desk. Guns ranging from Derringers, to larger bore Magnums, with samples of ammunition under each weapon. In the corner of the room, there was a large safe, large enough to house an assortment of long guns, assault rifles and the like, with a sign of Do Not Touch in bright orange against a white background, over the large combination lock in bright silver.

Chapter Twenty-Four

The fog was thicker than usual. Lew walked on, unknowing what destination he was heading for. Grey walls of fog were surrounding him. It did not appear to faze him. He went on . . . nothing he could do deterred him.

Further on there were four boys, teenagers, almost men, and they were flailing at something on the ground. One boy had about four feet long piece of 2x4 board, and was swinging it down in chopping strokes. Another assailant had a length of chain and was swinging it down on the form on the ground. The other two were just standing there observing the action.

Lew heard sounds like giggling from the group, along with the grunts of the two who were taking turns beating the inert lump in the dirt.

There was no letup in the action, as Lew came near. One of the giggling boys looked up and said something to the three others. The beating stopped, as they all turned around and faced him, standing in threatening positions. The chain in the one boy's hand was being swung back and forth. The 2x4 was being held like a baseball bat across the other boy's chest.

Lew did not stop approaching until he was directly in front of the two with the weapons.

"You better not take another step, mister," the bat boy said in a voice that broke, just as if his voice was still changing.'

"Yeah," the chain wielder said in a low voice.

Lew looked down at the hardly recognizable figure on the ground. "What is that?" Lew asked.

"That…is none of your business, old man," the voice changer rasped.

"Yeah," again the chain wielder echoed.

"And if you want some of what she's had you can still have some and maybe… more", said one of the standby kids said.

"I don't think so. As a matter of fact, I think if you value your lives you should drop those weapons and get down on your knees."

"Oh, ha, ha, ha. You're funny old man, and why would you think we should do that?"

"Well, I think you should think clearly. You don't have a choice. Either you do that or suffer the consequences", Lew said, his voice an eerie quiet.

"The, er, consequences. What consequences old man?" the chain holder said as he started to swing his weapon threateningly towards Lew.

Lew's hand flashed, the chain disappeared from the boy's grasp and landed four feet behind Lew.

"Wha, what happened?" the dazed boy gasped.

"That's one of the consequences I spoke about," Lew said.

"Okay, old man. That was very cute. But it's still four against one, and I think we can take you", said the board kid as he turned to his friends, "How about it guys?"

"Well, er, I think so" one of the observers said, a little hesitantly.

"Yeah, I think we can take him", the other observer piped up.

"That's only three of us, what about you?" the board boy turned to the ex-chain wielder.

"Did you see what he did, Chris? He took my chain and I didn't even see or feel it man. That was way cool.'

"Is that a 'yes' or a 'no', Bradley?"

Bradley was in a quandary, he didn't seem to know which way to turn. He looked at Lew, who stood at ease in front of the four of them and then back at the boy named Chris, who was posturing as if he was not afraid, and at Brian and Michael, the other two boys who he could not read.

"Well," Lew said, completely calm, knowing that two or three of the boys were on the fence, and that the boy called Chris was virtually alone out there.

"I don't think you have a choice anymore, Chris. Your pals are not about to back your play, so make it easy on yourself," Lew said coldly.

"Oh, yeah, well I know them a little better than you, old man", Chris said as he took a step forward and swung the board at Lew's head.

Lew stepped to the left as the board whistled past his head, missing by about a foot.

Swinging back, the board whooshed past Lew's head again, and with one swift move Lew's hand closed around Chris's right hand. He twisted to the right and before Chris knew it, the board bounced across the side of his head with a thud. He dropped to his knees, his hands holding both sides of his head in obvious pain.

"Don't say I didn't warn you, Chris," Lew said, not a bit out of breath.

All at once, the other three boys dropped to their knees and looked up at Lew.

"What are you going to do to us?" one boy cried.

"First, I'm going to see what you did to this girl", he pointed to the boy named Brian. "Come over here and help me turn her over."

Chapter Twenty-Five

The form moaned as Lew and Brian turned her over, her face was badly bruised, with chain marks across her cheeks, her lips were bloodied and two teeth protruded from her mouth, her body was covered with a sweatshirt emblazoned with the Arthur High School cheerleader's emblem. Her sweat pants had been pulled down almost to her knees and sported several tears along the front.

"Please, no more", the girl croaked, barely able to speak from the pain in her mouth and her cracked lips.

"It's okay," Lew said, "They won't hurt you anymore."

"Why?" she whispered. "Why did they do this to me?"

"I don't know, but I'm going to find out," Lew said with conviction in his tone.

As he turned to confront Chris and the others, he saw they had taken off while he tended to the girl. Only Brian had remained behind, probably because Lew was too close to allow him to escape.

"Well, kid, apparently your brave friends have left you to take the fall for them. Some friends you have." Lew looked deep into Brian's eyes, seeing remorse for what he had done and regret that he had not taken off as his so-called friends had.

"They're not my friends. Only Michael is. The other two sort of embarrassed us into coming along, and I don't know why they picked on her."

"Well, you and Michael were standing there laughing while they were beating her. What's that all about?"

"I don't know, it was like, contagious. I couldn't help it."

"Is that why you couldn't stop it and try to help her?"

Lew pointed to the girl, who seemed to be about 15 years old.

"Believe me, mister. I just couldn't get up the courage to go up against Chris and Bradley. I just couldn't."

"Okay, kid. I'm going to call 911 and get an ambulance over here. I want you to stay right here and hold her hand until they get here. Don't worry I'm not leaving and neither are you."

Lew bent down to the girl and asked, "What's your name?"

"Martha," she moaned again as her face twisted in pain.

"Well, stay still. Help is coming and Brian will be here with you until they come. They will take you to the hospital and take care of you. Is that okay?"

She could only moan and nod her head slightly, and Lew took it as a yes.

As he went to stand, he felt her hand on his arm. He looked down as she motioned him to come closer, "Please sir, what is your name?" she managed to get out before she moaned and sucked in some of the blood on her lips.

"That's not important, Martha. You just relax and wait for the paramedics to come and take care of you," he said.

"But, who are you?"

"I'm nobody, just someone who came to help," Lew said as he disentangled her hand and rose to confront Brian once again.

"Brian, I'm trusting you to stay with her. Can I do that?"

Brian looked down at the injured girl and then turned to Lew, he looked directly into his eyes and said with complete earnestness, "Yes, sir. You can, I won't leave her, and I'll go to the hospital with her."

"I believe you will, Brian," Lew said and as he looked at the boy he saw a nicely dressed young man with a clean look about him, he judged him to be about 16 years of age with a neat haircut and a very honest, but remorseful face and an athletic body.

"But, sir. Who are you?"

"As I told the girl, I'm nobody, just somebody who saw the need to help."

As he said this, he heard the sirens coming closer, he grasped Brian's shoulder and said, "Stay away from those other boys, they're no good".

"Yes, sir," Brian said and somehow Lew believed him as he sauntered away and back into his fog.

Chapter Twenty-Six

Ralph and Alan responded with the paramedics' bus only a moment behind.

They observed a teenage boy crouched over the form of an injured girl as the first medic approached. The boy stood as the medic bent down to assess the damage. The other medic brought a gurney loaded with their equipment and stopped alongside the prone figure.

Ralph and Alan took up stations behind the paramedics and waited their turn, eager to ask the boy their questions.

"Miss," the first medic asked, "Can you tell us what happened?"

'I don't know, I was walking home from practice and something hit me on the back of my head, and before I knew it, they were hitting me, and I couldn't stop them."

"Who was hitting you?"

"Four boys."

"Four boys, do you know who they are?"

"No."

"Do you know why they were beating you?"

"No," she moaned.

Alan took Brian aside and asked, "Who are you?"

'My name is Brian."

"And what are you doing here?"

"I. er, was with the boys who did this to her, but I didn't touch her. I didn't hit her. I'm sorry about what they did."

"Do you know the names of those who did this?" Alan asked as he took out his note pad.

"I do."

"Well, do I have to pull this out of you or are you going to tell me now?"

"Chris Walter and Bradley Stone were the boys who were beating on her. Chris had a board and Bradley had a chain."

"What about the other one? She said there were four. Who was the other one?"

"Michael Richards, but he wasn't beating her. He and I were just watching," Brian said.

"You were just watching…what are you, a jerk, you were watching two boys beating a young girl, and you just stood there…watching?"

"Yes, sir. I don't know why, but the other guy that was here said I should have stopped them, but I was afraid".

"What other guy?"

The guy that took the chain out of Bradley's hand and took Chris's board away".

"A guy took a chain and a board away from your friends and you just stood and watched?"

"Yes, sir".

"Okay, let me get this straight. Two guys, boys, were beating this girl with a piece of wood and a chain. You and another friend just stood by and watched, right?"

"Yes, sir."

"And then, someone came along and disarmed Chris and Bradley."

"Yes, sir."

"But, you don't know who this person is?"

"Yes, sir."

"Yes, you know who he is?"

"No, sir. I don't know who he is."

"Okay, let me go over this one more time," and Alan repeated everything that was said. "Do I have all of this right?"

"Yes, sir".

"Okay, stay here. Don't move", Alan ordered.

"Yes, sir".

"And please, stop saying sir."

"Okay, sir", Brian said hanging his head.

Alan walked over to Ralph while he was overseeing the medics tending to the girl.

"Ralph, we got a guy who disarmed two perps and when he went to see about her", Alan pointed to the battered girl. "Three boys took off, and this one, Brian, stayed with her. He's been very forthcoming with information, but he doesn't know the guy who came to her rescue."

"Alright, we'll take him back to the station and have his statement typed up and signed. Did he identify the other boys?"

"Yep, he did. "

The paramedics transferred the girl to their bus and prepared to take her to the Arthur Hospital when Ralph approached and asked about her condition.

Greg Smith, the prime medic said, "She's pretty badly banged up, but they can help her more at the hospital. You'll get a full report as soon as we get a minute. We're taking off now."

"Okay, good job guys."

"Thanks, that's the job is all", he said as he climbed behind the wheel and slowly drove off.

"Okay, Al. Let's get this youngster back to the station", as he put Brian carefully in the back seat of the car.

Chapter Twenty-Seven

They ran, looking back over their shoulders, hoping not to see the figure that had bested them while they were having such a good time beating the girl. None of the three had enough breath to talk while they ran, and they ran as if their lives counted upon it.

Just then, Chris pulled up, clutching his side, barely able to catch his breath.

"Wha, what the hell happened back there?" he rasped, "Who the hell was that sumofabich?"

The other two pulled up, Bradley dropped heavily to the ground, wincing in a searing pain in his side and panting heavily.

Michael stood leaning against a tree, his head swimming with exhaustion.

Bradley finally regained his voice, "I don't know man, but he sure is fast for an old dude, did you see?" he gasped. "See how he grabbed the chain, man? I never saw it coming."

"Yeah," Chris moaned "And he hit me with the board. I never even felt him take it away."

Michael piped up, "I'm out of here, you guys better get somewhere fast". and he turned and ran away.

"Oh jeez, Chris, what do you think we should do? That guy will probably call the cops."

"Brad, I don't know what you're going to do, but I'm taking Mike's suggestion and getting the hell out of here. You do what you think you should do, but I'm going it alone. I don't need no company."

"Chris, tell me what to do, please, my head is spinning, I can't think straight."

"Okay, I'll tell you what I'm gonna do, but you can't go with me."

"Sure, sure, just help me out here. What're you going to do?"

"Well, I'm going to the city"

"You mean New York?"

"Damn, you are stupid. Yes, I mean New York. And, I'm gonna get myself lost there. Don't even think you're coming with me, you hear?"

"Yeah, yeah, I hear you. But how are you going to live, we don't got no money."

"I'll make out. I got skills. I'll make out," Chris said, not sure he sounded confident.

"Okay, Chris. I hope you do make it. I don't know what I'm going to do, yet."

"Just don't hang around here, Brad. They'll be looking for you. And if one of those kids, Brian or Michael talks your ass is grass, you get it Brad?"

"Brian and Mike, I hadn't thought about them. What do you think they're going to do? Do you think they're going to talk?"

"I don't know about that Brian kid, but Mike said he's leaving town. I haven't hung around Brian, but he stayed behind when that guy chased us off. I don't know man. I just don't know. Anyway I'm leaving…now!!!"

Bradley watched, his mind reeling, as Chris loped off and disappeared around a house on the street.

He turned around, and around, and once more before slowly walking down the middle of the street. He heard sirens sounding a little ways away, getting louder. He walked just a little faster.

Chapter Twenty-Eight

Over 250 years ago, on the very site of the town of Arthur, there lived a civilization of Indians called the Sentero. The Sentero Indians were a peaceful and productive people. They lived without war, without crime, and without petty jealousies.

For centuries, their lives were uneventful and they were a happy people.

It came upon them--it seemed in a flash. Gases from far below the surface drifted upwards. The entire community was wiped out, men, women, children, pets, and all the livestock that inhabited the area.

Centuries later, people gravitated to the site, unaware of the past debacle that had occurred there. Some amateur archeologists had probed certain areas where a few artifacts had been unearthed in the process of digging foundations for future homes.

Skeletons of animals and birds that and stratified years ago began to show up, but these amateurs had no expertise to establish what had happened years ago.

Throughout the ensuing years, the gasses that had permeated the site had dissipated to a great degree, but underneath Lew Wallace's home there appeared to be long buried pocket still alive.

The seepage was not sufficient to kill, but it seemed to have an adverse effect on Lew's inner cortex. So much so that the fogs that Lew experienced came directly from these small amounts.

No one else in Lew's house had been affected, but something in his brain makeup had been. And, although it had not affected his daily life, it was only when the fog came did Lew change. It did not make him overly violent, but it did appear to heighten his sense of decency to a point that he found that he either was somehow directed to areas where violence was about to happen or was happening at that very time. Hence his proclivity to be at the right time and the right place, to do something about it, and do something he usually did.

Chapter Twenty-Nine

There's something very strange going on in the town of Arthur", Ralph intoned ominously to Alan Beckman, "Something very strange".

"Yes, but what?" asked his partner, "All we know for a fact is that whenever someone is in trouble, strange things happen, and there's an appearance by some sort of, and I use the word 'VIGILANTE' hesitantly. Maybe all we have is a 'GOOD SAMARITAN' who is looking out for everyone. What do you think?"

"Well, Al. I would like to put some kind of name to it, but the fact of the matter is that there is a man in the hospital without a penis. I don't think 'Good Samaritan' fits the role. Maybe if the guy in the hospital would talk we could pin it down a little better, but he's keeping his mouth closed tight about everything. I think he's trying to be too macho in front of his pals."

"And now he's minus his manhood, some macho man he's going to be."

"And his biggest problem isn't the lack of parts. It's that if he was in the process of attacking a citizen of this town, all we have to do is get that person to press charges."

"Okay, Al. But, let's see if we can find this superman Samaritan."

"Let's see if the girls that were involved can shed some light on who he is. See if there's a sketch artist on the payroll of this town." said Ralph.

"First we need to get the girls in here."

"Right, the chief should be able to help there. Let's get together with him," Ralph said as they went in search of the man.

Chapter Thirty

The room was kept dark. No sunlight invaded the gloom. The clicking and beeping of the monitors attached to the girl's chest and arms were constant, indicating that all her vital signs were behaving normally.

Her eyes were swollen shut, her lips were split in two places and her right arm was broken but set in a plaster cast and was lying along her side.

A nurse was carefully taking her temperature and noting data on her chart.

A moan escaped her broken lips and her left hand stirred as if to grasp a little life.

"Shh" the nurse cautioned, "Don't try to speak. Try to relax. We're taking good care of you, lie still."

"Mmm", the girl tried to speak.

"Lie still. I'll get your doctor in here and you can try to speak to him."

She paged the resident on duty and waited silently for the reply.

"Where, where am I?" the girl managed to say.

"You're in the hospital. You're safe. Don't worry. Please don't try to talk. You've been badly beaten. But like I said, you are safe now."

"I'm safe?"

"Yes, you are. Your doctor will be here shortly and he will talk to you."

Outside the doctor spoke briefly to an officer who had been assigned to stand guard over the girl and then entered the room.

"Well, hello, young lady. I'm Doctor Melvin, I have been talking to the police, and your attack has been reported. There is a policeman stationed outside your room and no one will harm you here. Now tell me if you can, does this hurt?" he said as he palpated a portion of her chest.

"A, a little", she managed to say.

"Okay, nothing to worry about, just a little fluid over there, we'll get that taken care of."

He turned to the nurse, "How many units of glucose have you given her, nurse?"

"Just two, doctor. She's fairly stable now so we have her on a slow drip for now. If you want her to have more, we can do it."

"No, that's good. Now, miss, can you tell us your name? There was no ID on you when you were brought in."

"Martha," she mumbled, her face twisting slightly in pain.

"Okay, Martha. Is there anyone that we can contact? Anyone, like your parents or a friend?"

"Yes, my Mom."

"Okay, what is your last name? And, if you can give us a phone number where we can reach her, that'll be good, too."

Martha relayed the information haltingly, obviously still in a great deal of pain.

"Nurse, let the officer outside know and in the meantime I'll try to ease Martha's pain some more."

"Yes, Doctor" she said and stepped out to give the policeman the information.

"Now, Martha, can you remember what happened, the police will want you to give them a statement when you get a little better, do you think you will be able to do that, I mean, when you can?"

She tried to nod her head to indicate she would, but her head started to pound with the movement, "Ooh, my head", she moaned.

"Just take it easy, nothing is that important. You just have to rest right now. I'm going to give you something to make you sleep and ease your pain", he said as he injected a clear liquid into the intravenous tube in her arm."

"Sleep now, little Martha. I'll be back soon", he whispered and left the room silently.

Chapter Thirty-One

"We've got to put some sense to this, Al. Maybe, just maybe, this girl at the hospital can put a face on this mysterious stranger who appears and disappears at will, and for some reason no one so far has been able to identify him. Maybe no one wants to identify him because they think he's doing such good things. We've got to start canvassing the town, it shouldn't take long. We can't discount the school kids or any one that is out at night that might have seen him."

"I'll start with the store owners, they see everyone", Alan said.

"Okay and I'll go through the department's incident reports. Maybe they'll give me a hint as to prior events. Get together with me around four, unless you come up with something before then. I'll do the same."

"Good luck, Ralph, but I think I got the better end of the deal. At least I'm outside on the streets, I hate going through reports. It makes my head swim and my eyes tear up."

"Yeah, yeah, I hear you. It does the same to me, but somebody has to do it. Talk to you later, pal," Ralph said as he headed to the records room.

Alan hurried out of the station, checking his micro-recorder for fresh batteries, in case he caught a break and got some good intel.

It was the fall season, and the foliage was in full splendor. Alan smelled the fresh air fill his lungs as he started down the main street of the small town.

He looked up and down the street and noted ten to fifteen stores of various sizes lining both sides of the street with the largest being the sporting goods store that was approximately in the center of all of them.

"A good place to start, since the recent break in and violence occurring there," Alan said to himself as he headed in that direction.

He was stopped on his way by a rather smallish heavyset man who almost knocked him over coming out of the town's single barbershop. The man smelled of English Leather cologne and he had a sprinkling of talcum powder across his shoulders.

"Uhh, sorry. I didn't see you there," the man said.

"That's okay. I guess I was daydreaming and wasn't paying attention," Alan said as he held out his hand, "I'm Detective Alan Beckman".

The pudgy little man grasped his hand in his chubby little hand and pumped it twice, "Detective, huh, I guess you're here to solve the store's problems," he said as he indicated the sports store with his thumb.

"Among other things that are happening around here lately. What do you think happened over there?" Alan said nodding towards the store. He turned his recorder on in his pocket with a touch of a button.

"All I know is there's someone who's supplanting the police force and taking things into his own hands and thank goodness for him. The young girls in this town are scared stiff and I blame the bicycle gang at the end of town. It's about time they were taken down and gotten rid of. They get what they deserve."

Alan responded by saying, "No one should take the law into his own hands, whether or not it's right. It's always wrong and sooner or later, it will come back and bite them. And by the way, what was your name, sir?"

"Oh, I'm Bob Franks. I'm an accountant. I have an office on the second floor over the antique shop, over there," he said as he pointed to a store halfway down the street.

"Well, Bob, do you have any idea who this Good Samaritan might be?"

"Er, no, I don't really, but if you find him I sure would like to shake his hand. Listen, I've got to go, business you know. Well nice to meet you, Detective, and good luck with your search," he said as he scurried away, looking once or twice over his chubby shoulder.

"Yeah, nice meeting you, too," Alan said to himself as he thumbed the recorder off "I think you know more than you are saying, Bob Franks."

Alan stared down the street again, hoping to bump into someone else that would be more forthcoming than his new chubby friend had been.

Chapter Thirty-Two

Bernie Tampon faced a semi-circle of his brother bikers' faces that registered both anger and incredulous frowns. He thought his position as their new leader had been cemented with the advent of Bobby's possible demise at the hands of a person who had cut off his manhood and dumped him beside his motorcycle at the entrance to the hospital.

Not one of the bikers had doubted Bernie's story that he had left Bobby's company earlier that evening, but they appeared to be questioning his story that the stranger who had made Bobby lose his cool and self-respect the other night was to blame.

All Bernie would say was that Bobby did not seem to be himself since that confrontation.

"Bernie, you don't think that guy cut Bobby's thing, do you?" Chaz Fenton, a rather filthy, hairy faced biker asked.

"I can't say, Chaz. I just don't know, but who else is there?"

"No way, man", a voice from behind the circle piped up.

"Yeah," chorused the rest of the bikers "That dude can talk, but we don't think he's a knife user."

"But, then who could do it?" Bernie asked.

"Maybe it was one of the Cross," Chaz said.

The Cross were a rival biker gang that was looking to take over the territory. They were a particularly violent gang that had its eyes on Bobby for a long time. On many occasions, the Cross had imposed their presence on Bobby's turf. They had more or less copied the M.O. (modus operandi) of Bobby's gang, thereby causing more trouble than his gang had engendered.

The leader of the Cross gang was a smaller than small person named Enos Pickerel, whose gang name naturally was Enis the Penis. Naturally, because it was reputed that Enis' penis was unnaturally large for a man who stood no higher than 5'1" tall.

Despite his size, Enis was considered the meanest member of the Cross gang, all who sported a rhinestone cross across the back of their jackets and on various assortments of their helmets.

Any mention of his diminutive size caused a knife-wielding rampage that could only be eased by bloodletting of the guilty party. That party could be a gang member or might be a passerby who had the balls to say something disparaging.

Enis coveted Bobby's height and bulk, besides his gang, and as any person of such small size (e.g. Hitler, Napoleon, etc.) needed the power to assuage his paranoia.

It came to Bernie's knowledge that it might have been Enis who waylaid Bobby when he was a bit under the influence; cold cocked him, and took the opportunity to emasculate him by slicing off the aforementioned part.

"Guys", Bernie addressed the gang, "We have to take our revenge on Bobby's attacker, in particular…Enis the Penis".

"Whoa, Bernie," Frank Jacks, a bald, well-tattooed member said from the middle of the group, "Let's not jump the gun here, the Cross is not a gang to take lightly, they outnumber us three to one and we don't know for sure it was Enis. Do we?"

"Right", Jerry Falco, another member spoke up, "We could be making a big mistake, you know. It might have been someone else. Maybe that guy Bobby ran into the other night. You know, that guy that faced him down in the park.

"Hmm, you might be right, Jerry. But he didn't look like the kind of guy who could handle a knife good enough to do that to Bobby", someone else from the gang added.

"Well, we've gotta figure who else could have done this. Bobby is still unconscious, and even if he wakes up, he may not want to tell us who done this. He may want to either forget it, something I don't think he can or wants to do, and he may want to take care of this himself in his own way. Either way, we gotta watch our own backs. And I don't have to tell youse guys, nobody talks to the cops, got it?" Bernie said strongly.

Chapter Thirty-Three

Alan progressed down the street, stopping in at some of the shops that were still open. It was getting on to 5:30 in the afternoon and quite a few of the stores had closed for the day.

At a real estate office, there was one person still in attendance. She was a rather dowdy middle-aged woman dressed in a brown skirt with a beige blouse and sensible wedged shoes that matched her skirt.

She wore oversized reading glasses perched on the end of a nose that had seen more than one martini over too long a time. Otherwise, she was not unusual in any other way.

Alan walked in and presented himself with his badge and a warm smile.

"Good afternoon, ma'am. I'm Detective Alan Beckman. May I take a moment of your time?"

"Good afternoon, Detective. Of course, you may. What can I help you with?"

"Well, ma'am," Alan said as he took the seat opposite her across her desk, which was littered with real estate brochures. "I'm here upon the request of your mayor. I'm looking into the recent rash of violence in town."

"Hmm, I know what you are talking about. How is it you think I can help?"

"Well Miss, or is it Mrs.?" Alan asked, as he could not determine her marriage status, her hand was below her desk.

"It's Mrs. Campbell, Marge," she said smiling at his discomfort.

"Well, Mrs. Campbell, we have heard that there is someone in this town that does things, good things, for people and does those things anonymously. Have you heard of him?"

She sat for more than a few minutes, not moving, looking directly into Alan's eyes, tears starting to form at the corner of hers.

"Mrs. Campbell, is there anything wrong? Is it something I said?" Alan said sliding forward in his chair.

"Oh, no," she said "It's just that the person you are talking about is one of the most respected and honorable people in this town."

"Okay, Mrs. Campbell. Don't cry. We only want to talk to this person. We're not looking to cause him any trouble. We need to find out how he knows about where the troubles are about to happen."

More tears streamed down her face, she started to tremble slightly, and her hands were shuffling through the brochures on her desk as if she could not control them. She looked away from Alan's probing eyes.

"Detective, I can't help you. I would like to be able to, but without getting permission from this person I would not want to give out his name. I'm so sorry, can you understand?"

"Actually…no, I don't understand anyone who is not willing to cooperate with the authorities. But, don't you worry, Mrs. Campbell. We will find this person and I'm really sorry I made you cry," Alan said in a conciliatory way.

"I'll leave you now so you can get back to what you were doing, but I'm really disappointed in you."

He handed her his card and said, "If you find you want to talk to me, please don't hesitate to call."

She reached out with a shaky hand and took his card with down cast eyes. Alan turned and left the office, smiling, almost pleased with himself.

Chapter Thirty-Four

Lew was busy at work when Alan strolled into the store, Lew recognized him from the night before when the two New York detectives were investigating the carnage that had taken place in the store.

He made himself invisible behind a rack of baseball equipment, but watched every move the detective made. Lew was not afraid of speaking with him, but preferred not to be in the forefront when the questions started.

Lew watched as Alan spoke to the manager, his friend, and went from point to point looking and listening to what the manager and his staff had to do to get the store ready for the morning's business. He had kept the customers from getting too close to the crime scene tape that separated the grisly scenes from the rest of the store.

"Lew, Lew, where are you?" the manager called out, "Lew, I need you over here", He called out again.

Against his better judgment, Lew called out himself, "I'm over here, Bob. I'm back here in the baseball section. Wait a minute. I'll be right there."

Alan turned his back to where Lew's voice had come from and asked, "Who is Lew?"

"He's my assistant manager. Nice guy, he'll be right with us."

"Oh, and do you know what time he closes the store at night?"

"Sure, we close every night at seven always. Lew closes on the dot, except if he has a customer that needs his help. He's the best salesman I have and the nicest man I would say in this whole town. He has helped so many people in so many ways. I have to tell you he's the town hero."

"How so? I've spoken to a lot of people and his name has never come up, until now."

"Well, Lew doesn't crow about all the things he has done, but he's been lauded by the mayor and almost everybody in town. Let's face it, everybody pretty much knows everybody else's business here. Lew is modest. But trust me, he's the best."

"Okay, you've convinced me. Now where is he? I'd like to meet the best man in town."

"Oh, Lew, where are you?" Bob Martin called out again.

"Right here, Bob," Lew said, startling both Alan and Bob by coming up behind them.

"Lew," Bob said as he caught his breath, "This is Detective Alan Beckman. He has some questions about what happened here."

"Oh, hi, Detective," Lew said as he held his hand out, shaking Alan's.

"Anything I can do to help. What exactly do you need to know?"

Alan wanted to ask him some completely different questions, but was not about to tip his hand. He suspected that Lew was the man they were searching for, but he needed more time and more corroboration of his suspicions before confronting him now.

He simply went on and said, "I know you weren't here when this happened, were you?"

"Why, no. I closed at seven. I guess I was home when this was going on."

"Is there anything that you could see when you were called in that doesn't look right to you? I mean, unusual?"

"The whole thing looked unusual. The place was clean and neat when I left, but when I was called this morning, it looked like all hell was let loose in here. I can tell you it won't be back to normal for quite a while. There's a lot to clean up, I can tell you."

"I see," said Alan, "Who do you think would do this? I know we found a body, but so far, we haven't been able to identify it. Do you know anybody from the biker gangs?"

"Not personally, but some of them come in here occasionally, for parts and helmets," Lew said.

"Hmm," Alan mused "But you don't know any of them outside of the store that come in here?"

"No, Detective. I don't travel in those circles."

"Was there anything missing from the break-in? I mean, that you can tell?"

I'm sure there is, but we haven't taken inventory yet. That will take some time."

"Okay, can I get your name and information?"

"Sure, let's go back to my office and I'll give you what you need."

As Alan and Lew started to go, Alan said to Bob Martin, "I'll be right back and we'll talk more."

"Okay, Detective. I'll be around. You'll be able to get me anytime."

"Thanks," Alan said as he followed Lew to the back of the store.

Chapter Thirty-Five

Reports from the forensic lab came back and Ralph slid the files over the small desk that had been provided by the Arthur P. D. to Alan.

Alan shrugged out of his jacket, straightened his tie, fished his glasses out of his breast pocket, and studied the report.

"Ralph," he remarked, "Do you notice how many prints are on this thing? We may have to print half the town. There must be a dozen different ones", he chuckled as he said this.

"I know, Al. But, the most prevalent ones are those that belong to the employees and the assistant manager. It makes sense those are there, so we can, and should, omit them, unless we find a weapon with any of their prints on it."

"Right, but the others have to be the prints of the ones who broke in and, uh, whoever took out that guy in the rubble. I don't think we can discount anyone right now."

"Al, did you find out anything in your interviews on Main Street, I know you stopped into almost every shop and office down there."

"Well, yes, I did. Almost to a man or woman, they all had really glowing things to say about this Lew Wallace, the assistant manager at the sports store. They all say that ever since they have known him, and some go back to his childhood, he has done so many good things. He was born and grew up here in Arthur."

"Hmm, a do-gooder, eh" Ralph mused.

"Yeah, just that. No one remembers anything that he has done that has not had a good or beneficial result."

"Pretty strange, don't you think, Al?"

"You have a very suspicious mind, Ralphie. Why are you so dubious about this guy?"

"I don't know, but he seems too good to be true."

"Come on, why does he make you think that way?" Alan was trying to feel Ralph out, hoping that he would shed some light on the way he was thinking. Lew Wallace was the hero of the town and he was very much, in Alan's mind, the prime suspect in the vigilante actions.

"Oh, I don't know," Ralph, said again, "But if it doesn't make sense…" he did not finish his statement but his brow furrowed as if deep in thought.

Alan looked at his partner in confusion. He got up, strolled over to the window, and looked down Main Street wondering what Ralph had in his mind that he was not saying.

"Ralph, just what are you not saying? I don't understand. Do you want to bring this Wallace in?"

"What I'm saying is that sometimes someone is just too obvious to ignore. And yes, I'd like to talk to this Lew Wallace."

Chapter Thirty-Six

Fifteen miles away in the big city, Lew wandered the streets. He was looking for a church, no one in particular, just a church. He knew he could not go to his parish in Arthur to achieve what he was seeking. He knew though that in Manhattan he could be virtually anonymous. His goal was to speak to someone who did not know anything about him or his family or background, and bare his soul and attempt to make some sense of it all.

Street after street did not yield the object of his search. He thought he might have to go deep into the heart of the city before he found the perfect place. But, as he turned the corner, he saw two large oak doors that belonged to a moderate sized house of worship.

On wobbly legs, he climbed the four granite steps that led to the entrance. He glanced up and the huge cross atop the building somehow gave him the needed strength to pull the doors open and enter the church.

He was met with warm quiet. The muted lighting from the nave that housed the votive candles drew him deeper into the body of the church. Half of the candles were lit and flickering in the dimness of the nave.

He walked down the center aisle slowly, reverently looking from right to left at the statues in niches along the walls.

He took a seat in the second row of pews, genuflected a moment, and then sat back with his eyes closed.

As he sat there, thoughts of what he had been going through raced through his head like a movie reel gone amok. He shook his head, trying to shake those thoughts away.

A soft rustle beside him brought him out of his reverie. He slowly opened his eyes and looked around. He turned to his right and discovered a young, blond haired man in a grey shirt and trousers with the traditional white insert in his collar.

"Hello," Lew said in a quiet voice.

"Hello, I'm Father Joely," the man said, "I've never seen you before, do you need anything? Is there anything I can do for you?"

"I think so, Father. I need to speak to someone, but I'm not sure if there is anyone who will be able to help me."

"I don't know if I can help, but I can try. The Lord does work ways that no one really understands, but if you believe…" he left his words trail on.

"I'm trying to do that, Father. But it's so difficult, I mean, the things that are happening to me", he shrugged his shoulders "I just don't know".

Father Joely looked at Lew, sitting there, definitely distressed, a look on his face that was obviously tormented.

"Sir, I don't know your name, and as you can see, I'm a lot younger than you, but my calling says that I must try to help you make sense of your problem. Perhaps you can tell me just what it is, and if I can't help, I can get the church elder, and he might be better able to help. Do you want me to do that?"

"No, no, please don't. If I can just talk to you it might, maybe help. Would that be okay with you?"

"Of course, I would be happy to try to help."

Lew went on to tell the priest everything that he was experiencing. It took the better part of the morning. Father Joely listened intently, at some points he asked a question, but let Lew tell his story virtually non-stop.

As Lew came to the present and his finding the priest's church, the father became silent. His silence found Lew staring at his unlined face, wondering if his story was too much for someone so ill equipped in human suffering to be able to make sense of it all.

After what seemed a long time, the priest looked up at Lew and said, "Sir, there are so many things that happen in a person's life that defies explanation, but I can say that what you have been going through is not necessarily a bad thing. Confusing, I admit, but you appear to have been doing only good things in this, how can I phrase it, your fugue state. I'm not a doctor, but that's what I think it would be called."

"But, Father, I don't know, maybe I have done things and not remembered them. How am I supposed to know?"

"That's not an answer I can give to you, sir. I only know that that is where you have to have faith and that faith will be your guidance and the hope you will continue to do only good. I can't give you any guarantees, but you must be true to yourself."

Lew turned to the young prelate with tears in his eyes, and in spite of the warmth of the church, he shivered slightly.

His eyes took in the young priest and slowly his look took in the simplicity of the church. He looked at the figure of Christ on the cross above the altar. The countenance of the figure held him in its gaze and he felt a calm wash over him, not providing him an answer but providing a sort of solace within him.

He turned back to the priest and softly said, "Thank you, Father. I think I can go home now. I appreciate your words and your time."

"You're welcome, sir. I don't feel comfortable saying my son… but you can understand that, I know."

"Yes, Father. And thank you again", Lew said as he rose and made his way up the aisle and out of the large oak doors into the bright sunlight.

He blinked once and left the area feeling better than when he came.

Chapter Thirty-Seven

After agreeing to speak to Lew, Ralph and Alan continued to discuss the fact that Lew Wallace was the most obvious choice for the stranger who steps in at the most opportune moments.

"I don't think that he doesn't have an agenda and that all of these people only see what he might want them to see. Something doesn't ring true, is all that I'm saying."

"Okay, Ralph, but what if it turns out that he is a vigilante. Is that necessarily a bad thing?"

"No, it's not a bad thing, but what if he is the perp that did in the biker at the sporting goods store? You know he has a sort of vested interest there and that's murder, my friend. A step above a simple vigilante move."

"I see what you're getting at, partner. Let's go now before they close and have a serious talk with him."

"You got it Al, let's do it. We don't need to haul him in here yet. We can do it at the store."

With that, the two detectives snapped the file closed, pushed back their aluminum chairs, and swung out the front doors of the station.

At the same time the two detectives left the station, Lew was entering the store. He glanced to the left where there were three bare-chested workers untangling the racks that had been thrown aside and mingled together by the police in their attempt to find evidence in the murder of the now identified biker who was found in the back of the store.

"Bob", Lew called out to the manager, "How long do they expect to take to get this place ready for full business?"

Bob Martin was overseeing the operation from his office that looked out across the entire scope of the store.

"It should be done within the hour, as long as those New York detectives give us the clearance."

"Oh well, maybe it will be sooner than later. I see them coming down the street right now."

"Great, I hope they can give the okay now," Bob said nodding to Lew.

Ralph and Alan pushed through the doors and approached the two men.

"Good morning, gentlemen", Ralph said eyeing Lew. "I'm glad you're both here. We need to talk to both of you."

"Well, you've got a captive audience, Detectives. Ha, ha, that's a joke, Detectives", Bob said with a smile on his face.

"Yeah, quite a joke Mr. Martin. We get it," Al said with a serious look on his face "Now, may I speak to you alone?"

"Of course, come into my office," Bob said, starting back to the side stairwell.

"Mr. Wallace, I need to have your attention over here." Ralph indicated to one of the checkout counters.

Lew nodded and followed Ralph the few feet to the counter.

"Can I ask you if you can clear the place so we can open sometime today detective?" Lew asked.

"I think that can be arranged, Mr. Wallace. But I need to ask you a few questions first."

"Okay, but give me a minute. I have to check my staff in and give them their instructions first. Otherwise they'll just stand around doing nothing."

"Go right ahead. I'll be waiting right here," Ralph said pointing to a corner where workout machines were organized in a neat row.

Ralph watched as Lew ambled over to three salespeople and began pointing to various areas in the store. After a few minutes, they broke up and each went to their assigned task.

Lew walked back to Ralph and motioned him to his office, they both went in, and Lew took a seat behind his desk while Ralph decided to stand to the side of the desk. He leaned in and said, "Mr. Wallace, where were you when this went down?"

"I don't know where I was since I don't know when this thing happened, sir." Lew said as he looked up into Ralph's waiting face.

"You haven't been told what time this happened?"

"Well, it appears this happened after nine o'clock last night, you were here at that time?"

"No, I close and go home at seven. The store was closed by Mr. Martin last night."

"Do you know if he closed at that time?"

"I would assume so, he is very punctual."

"There couldn't be a customer here that would cause him to stay later?"

"I don't remember any time ever, since I've worked here, and I've worked here for a lot of years. It never has happened like that, ever."

"But you wouldn't know it if it did happen, would you?"

"I guess not."

"So, getting back to where you were last evening, Mr. Wallace."

"Please call me Lew. I don't think anyone calls me Mr. Wallace."

"So, Lew, where were you?"

"As far as I know I was home by 7:15. It doesn't take me long to get home. I passed the barber shop and the bakery on my way home."

"So, if I ask them to verify it they will agree?"

"Yes, I believe so, Detective. Am I a suspect here? The tone of your questions seems to indicate that." Lew said.

"At this time we have to consider everyone a sort of suspect. I'm only trying to find out what happened."

"I guess, but if you ask around, I'm sure you will find that I am very punctual."

"Okay, Lew. I think that'll be all for now. If need be I'll be back in touch. Thanks for your time."

Lew watched as Ralph threw him a half salute and left the office.

"Hmm," Ralph said to himself, "Too cooperative, very suspicious."

Chapter Thirty-Eight

Bernie Tampon stood with his back to the hardwood bar, his face a brilliant crimson, spittle foaming at the corner of his mouth. His eyes were bloodshot and his shoulders trembled with apparent rage.

He shouted above the TV that was blasting heavy metal rock music, "Shut off that damn TV. Shut it off now!!!"

Slowly one of the bikers rose and turned it down to a tolerable level as he eyed Bernie's face that was downright scary.

"Okay," Bernie yelled, still livid. "Bobby is in the hospital, as you all know. But, he's not talking yet. We all know that he got his dick cut off, whatever. But, what we don't know, but can guess at, who the cutter is. It can only be the Cross. They've been looking to get Bobby alone. It's only a miracle that he's not dead. The question is…what do we do about it?"

A loud babble erupted from the eleven men in the gang all at once.

Bernie's face turned a natural shade, seeing as how he had gotten such a response from the gang.

"Whoa, not all at once," he yelled. "Let's get some good ideas. I know you all want to avenge him, but we gotta think clearly. No use going off halfcocked or we'll not get anything done. Do you read me?"

Every one of them raised their fist and shouted, "Yeah".

"Okay, what we need is a plan, let's not rush into anything. We know where they hang out, that old barn on Route 3. But, it's in such a place that they can see us from any direction. Does anybody have any ideas?" Bernie said to the group.

There was a silence so thick you could cut it with a dull axe.

Mumbles from one corner gave birth to a comment from one of the members. Jason Mason, nicknamed the Bricklayer, muttered, "Well, er, maybe, um".

"Come on, Bricklayer, spit it out. If you got an idea let's hear it.

"Well, I was thinking."

"Oh, yeah, the Bricklayer was thinking", Alex Baker, nicknamed Doughboy, sarcastically intoned.

"Up yours, Doughboy. I do have an idea. Listen, we have to hit them at night, but we can't go in with our bikes", Jason the Bricklayer said in a huff.

"Bricklayer has a good idea there, but there's only one drawback, we have someone here that's a rat!!! It's somebody who's giving up our plans to the Cross. I hope it's not one of you. Because if it is, I promise, you're a dead man.

"No, no, it can't be one of us. Can it Bernie?" Jason piped up.

"I hope it's no one in this room, if it is..." He left this thought linger unspoken, but the intent was clear to all of them.

"Let's see, whose not here? Hmm", He mused, "Besides Bobby Pearl, there's Charlie Katz (the Pussy), Grant Forbes (500), Gene Rose (Flowers) and Jimmy Rolle (Bagels). One of them could be the stoolie, but I hope not. I like all of them."

"Yeah, we like all of them, too. But do we know who they know and who they talk to." The group all started to talk at once again.

Bernie held up his hand for quiet and said, "Okay, I need two of you to follow me into the back room. Er, Bricklayer and Doughboy come with me, the rest of you talk among yourselves."

As the three left the room the others looked at each other, unable to put together a salient thought and were left in virtual silence.

Bernie closed the door behind them and quickly turned facing the two burly men, "Tell me now, are either the two of you the rat!!!?"

Bricklayer and Doughboy turned two shades of white, their mouths both dropped open. "Bernie", Bricklayer sputtered, and "No, I swear it's not me. I swear it on my mother."

"Bull$#!+, Bricklayer. You ain't got no mother, she died when you was born. You told me so," Doughboy looked at him and stared him down.

"Damn, you're right. But, I swear on her grave, it's not me! How could I ever do that…never man."

"That doesn't absolve you or anyone. I can't leave it to anyone here to be sure I'm not giving the plan away. I just want you two to know that the plans are going to be in my head and you all will only know them when I say so. So you can tell them out there just what I said."

"Yeah, okay", they both said and left the room.

Chapter Thirty-Nine

There was no one to whom Lew could confide in. His wife was always there for him, but he was so confused he could not possibly explain what had been happening to him and he did not want to inflict any more pain on her. His head was in a tumult. What if he had done or would do something hurtful to someone during these fog times. What would he do? Forget about the fact that he was unaware of the time, was to put it mildly, 'befogged' was more like it.

The knife that had been discovered by Linda in his pocket confused him mightily and he was torn between taking it to the police and ignoring it completely. But, being the man he was, his decision ultimately was to take it to the authorities.

Then again, he believed that they held him in some suspicion, but to what extent he did not know and could not venture a creditable guess.

"Oh, well, I guess it's about time I got this over with", he said to himself as he approached the town's police station.

He walked in and faced a chest-high counter with a gate in the middle, to provide access to the large room beyond that was equipped with three desks where preliminary interviews were conducted.

A uniformed female officer sat on a stool with a large record book open before her. She looked up as Lew walked in and strode directly up to her.

"Can I help you, sir?" she asked, looking him up and down, as if to ascertain whether he had anything that could be construed as a weapon.

"I think so," Lew said, "I understand you have detectives from the city here, er, Bloom and Beckman."

"Yes, sir", she answered, "But can I help you…sir?"

"Well, I think I need to speak to either one of them. I may have something that can help with their case."

"May I have your name, sir," she said holding a pen ready to record his name.

"Lew Wallace."

"Okay, Mr. Wallace, please have a seat over there and I'll page them for you", she pointed to a row of chairs against the wall.

"Thank you, Officer."

"What if they think I used the knife myself? What if I did? Stop it", he chastised himself, "Stop it. You're doing the right thing, Lew."

"Mr. Wallace, Mr. Wallace", a deep male voice interrupted Lew's thoughts. "Mr. Wallace, please come in. Detective Bloom will see you now", a police officer called to him.

"Oh, yes. I'm sorry", Lew said to him as he got to his feet and moved to the open gate where the officer was standing.

"Please, follow me, sir."

Lew followed him through the room to a series of offices where the officer pointed to an open door.

"Right in there, sir. He'll be with you in a minute."

"Thank you", Lew said to the retreating back and went in and sat at the side of the only desk on the room. He looked around but did not see anything on the desk or on the filing cabinet against the sidewall.

After a few minutes Ralph walked in, "Good morning, Lew", he said.

Chapter Forty

The Cross Biker Club (Gang) was located a mile or so out of town. It was situated in the middle of a field in an old barn. Their bikes were almost always lined up in front of the structure, but in rainy weather, there was plenty of room inside to house their machines.

Ever since the invasion of the sporting goods store, they had opted to keep all their bikes inside and to assign a member to keep watch on both sides of the barn on a rotating basis, just in case either the cops or their rivals came calling.

Jose Penas aka Joey Peanuts was an older member of the ragtag club. Joey stood 5'11" and weighed over 250 lbs., most of which was total muscle, something that he used to intimidate his so-called brothers.

He usually wore denims, although it was difficult to discern that fact because he was mostly covered in grease from his neck to the hem of his jeans. His black studded boots were also caked with the offending grease and they squished as he walked. He wore his hair in a long braided ponytail with a bandana emblazoned with a silver cross dead center in front. His face had a filthy handlebar moustache and a brown flowing beard. A typical biker looks with a somewhat permanent sneer beneath the moustache.

It is typically assumed that people who are attracted to biker gangs, and or what they like to consider as CLUBS, are all the same ilk, but that is a false assumption. There are so many diverse personalities and motives involved in these types of clubs that one could not be correct in assuming that all bikers were evil or bad.

No club or gang could survive without different egos and motives.

Some clubs are devoted to just that, club activities for good and socially acceptable reasons. While the more notarized clubs, like the Hell's Angels, which by the way do many good things that are rarely reported, are known for how they are portrayed in the movies and on television in a negative way.

Socially unacceptable gangs give many good clubs a bad name and attract the sleaze element that look for the notoriety and profit from performing illicit and illegal acts.

Such are the two clubs that inhabit the town of Arthur.

The Cross has only one motive, to inflict as much harm and grief in that town and any other town it chooses to inflict itself upon.

Bobby Pearl's gang, while it hasn't formally branded themselves a proper name, has about the same thought process as the Cross. It is to be as non-conformist and socially unfit as the member's sick minds could be.

There might be, and it happens not often, some members of such clubs that do not embrace the mentality of the general misanthropic biker. They hide their feelings, and in an attempt to fit in, go along with the gang and change their look and way of speaking so as not to stand out and be ostracized. The worst thing they want is to be looked upon and branded as a creep.

So, now we look to the makeup of the Cross.

Chapter Forty-One

Enis the Penis's second in command went by the unlikely alias of The Professor. Hank Fellows does not follow the usual profile of a biker in that he is clean-shaven, well-groomed hair, and clean leather outfits, from leather vest to leather pants and highly shined combat boots.

He is well educated, with of all things, a degree in English literature, and an associate degree in psychology.

His motorcycle is kept highly shined and he only rides at the front of any group ride so as not to get dirty from all the dust kicked up by the other riders.

No tattoos or piercings adorn his body and he affects a pair of horned rimmed glasses under his goggles.

He does not involve himself in the more criminal aspects of the gang with the exception of planning the operations from the start to the necessary escape from these operations.

His obvious intellect has made a profound impact on the gang, in as much as he has a great influence on Enis the Penis. Not that he overrules Enis, but sometimes he can direct his more insane decisions, like to kill or maim someone who he thinks has done him a disservice or made an insult to his leadership or worst of all, his masculinity.

Hank is almost as formidable as Enis in that he stands a little over 6'4"tall but is as thin as a rail, giving him that lean and hungry look that intimidates most of his underlings.

He is believed to be as deadly as Enis, as his looks belie his manner.

Many of the others in the gang adhere to the belief that their looks should be as mean and vicious as a biker should be, bald heads and wild tattoo's, with every conceivable piercing adorned their bodies and clothing that runs the gamut from outright rags to various leather accessories. Chains around their necks and waists hung on almost all of them, except Hank, giving them the mean looks they were attempting to establish.

Chapter Forty-Two

"Well, Alan, what do you think? We have such a mob scene of suspects and not one idea who is the bad dude who killed the creep in the store and who sliced the other creep's dick off. I tell you pal, I'm stymied."

"So am I, Ralph. At one time, I see Lew Wallace and his fog story and at another time, we have the two groups with so many suspects. I don't know who or what happened to anyone."

"We know that the Cross is the gang that tossed the store. There's the knife that Lew turned over to us with no fingerprints, except his and his wife's prints. We also don't know until forensics comes back with the blood evidence, whose blood it is, the iced creep or the dickless one. Boy, Al, this is some jigsaw puzzle the Chief has thrown at us."

"It's a puzzle that keeps getting more pieces missing."

"I think we should get all the principles in here and do a little investigative head banging. Let's start with the leader of the Cross."

Ralph got together with the police chief and requested he send a couple of officers over to the Cross' barn and pick up Enis and his second in command plus one of the not so important members for questioning.

That done, Ralph and Alan put their heads together to map out a strategy.

"Al, you take the second in command and the peon. I'll take Enis the Penis into the main interrogation room and have at him. Do you have any idea who we should talk to after we get their statements and absorb their run-a-round."

"Possibly we should talk to Bernie Tampon and one of his pals after that. This doesn't let Lew off the hook, by any means."

"Okay, let's set up our rooms."

By 'this' Ralph meant that photos of the crime scene and Bobby Pearl's hospital situation, plus files that could be construed as important evidence, although they contained little or no information, but was good for window dressing.

It took nearly two hours before the Cross members were herded into the station and handed over to the two detectives.

"I want a lawyer," Joey Peanuts loudly pronounced, "And, I want one for each of my people".

"You can call your lawyer for yourself but you can't talk for anyone else," Ralph said calmly.

"Okay", he called to his two cohorts. "Youse guys know what to do."

"Right, Joey. I want a lawyer", said the peon.

"Yes," Enis said quietly, "I want a mouthpiece, also."

Ralph looked at Alan and whispered, "Damn, this is turning out to be some circus".

Alan just shrugged his shoulders and shook his head in agreement, as they herded their charges into their respective rooms.

Chapter Forty-Three

"Joey Peanuts, I pulled your sheet and I have to say I'm impressed. Petty theft, rape of under aged females, and, oh yes two 10-year olds. Yes, I know boys, an assault with a weapon. Yes, I know a wrench is not much of a weapon, but a weapon all the same. Last but not least, a DUI. Wow, Jose, with all these arrests one would think you'd be put away for a long, long time, but no!!! Here you are, sitting there with a &#!+ eating grin on your overly pockmarked face, looking like you got a free pass. You must have one helluva lawyer."

Joey Peanuts just sat there staring at Alan with that thousand-mile look on his face, as if he had put himself beyond Alan's reach.

"You don't have to say anything Jose, just listen. We know one of your guys was the body we found in the back of the sporting goods store. We also know that it is your gang."

"Club", Joey piped up all of a sudden. "We're a social club, not a gang."

"Okay, social club, whatever. But, we know it was your guys that were behind the break in and that you ran into something--something that ruined the job. What we would like to establish is what or who could do this to your…social club!!!"

"I ain't got nuthin' to say until my lawyer gets here."

"You 'ain't got nuthin' to say'. Man how and where did you learn to speak English, oh sorry, you're an alien. Where exactly do you come from, Jose?"

"They call me Joey, Joey Peanuts, man. And I don't gotta answer your questions, pal."

"First of all, Jose, I'm not your pal. I think you can count me as one of your enemies, Jose."

"I'm not talkin' no more", and with that he closed his eyes and slumped in his chair.

"Great, but I'm not, we have a subpoena for your barn, and, as we speak or not, Arthur's police are going through it with a fine-toothed comb and when they find what they're looking for. Your lawyer will have some job getting you off this time."

Joey nodded with his eyes still closed, "Yeah, Yeah."

Chapter Forty-Four

Lulu and her friend Sylvia sat close together and shook as if they were one person. They were in the office of Arthur's Chief of Police and were being scrutinized by a team of detectives that had come to town to back up Ralph and Alan.

"Ladies, we need to get your stories straight. My name is Detective Jimmy Chow and my partner here is Detective Elliot Smith.

"We're not here to make you say anything that will reflect in any way against you, but we want to know if you know anything about the man that helped you that day in the park."

Detective Smith said, "Yes, if you could describe him a little more distinctly it would be of tremendous help to us. We haven't been able to identify him yet."

"Well," Lulu said, "I know I was really scared and I was shaking really badly, but he looked like any older guy. He wore light brown pants, like khaki's and a blue shirt. He looked like any older guy you see on the street."

Detective Chow looked at Sylvia and asked, "Can you add anything else, Sylvia?"

She looked around the office and finally came to rest on Chow's baldhead. "To tell you the truth, I kept my eyes down on the ground. I was so scared they were going to hurt us I couldn't bear to look up. Even when the little guy showed up, I couldn't bring myself to look."

"But you didn't even see him when you were running away?"

"No, I didn't. I'm sorry."

"And you didn't either, Lulu?"

"No, I'm sorry."

"Okay, ladies, if you think of anything please don't hesitate to give us a call or come in", Chow said and handed each girl his card. "And, thank you for coming in."

Chapter Forty-Five

Alan had Kenny Budner aka Buddy, one of the other club members of the Cross biker 'club', in interrogation room number two. Buddy was obviously nervous being on his own in a room with a hardnosed looking detective and a burly uniformed Sheriff's officer.

He looked from Alan to the officer and back to Alan, his fingers beating an unknown tune on his black denim-covered knees. Sweat had broken out on his brow and there was a noticeable tic in his right eye.

Alan sat there and just stared at Buddy, he offered no comment, as did the uniformed officer.

They sat there for a good ten minutes, making Buddy more nervous by the minute.

The silent treatment reached a point that appeared to be too much for the biker.

"Man, ain't you gonna say sumthin'?" he pleaded, the tic more and more noticeable as he sat there, twitching and sweating.

Alan looked over to the officer and back at Buddy, still he said nothing.

"What the hell is goin' on? Man, what the hell are you doin'?" he practically yelled out, but at the last moment restrained himself, yet twitched even more.

Alan finally picked up the file folder that had been sitting on the metal table separating him from Buddy. He made like it was a long report and his eyes ran back and forth across the paper.

"What?" Buddy said, looking like a caged animal.

"Well...let's see," Alan finally said to the officer before he turned back to Buddy. Buddy's relief at someone saying something to him flooded over him like a refreshing waterfall.

"Kenny Budner, it appears you have been a very bad boy, hmm, rape, assault with a deadly weapon B&E, car theft, among many other things I haven't got time to go through. Oh, yeah, here it is. Major drug busts, using and selling. My, my Buddy you've been busy, haven't you?"

"Man, you got the wrong guy. I didn't do any of that stuff."

"Really, well here's your mug shot and your fingerprints. Prints that we found also at the sporting goods store, all over the place. Why didn't you wear gloves man?" and "Are you sure you want to go down that denial road, Buddy? Or, would you like to know just what I can offer you if you give me a statement about the job and your boss?"

"I don't know what you're talkin' about. What job and what boss?"

"Oh, I think you do Buddy, you see we have Joey Peanuts and Enis the Penis in the other rooms. And, if you know Joey, he doesn't take responsibility for anything. You know that, Bud?"

"What the hell are you talkin' about?" Buddy shouted.

"You know what I'm talking about," Alan said in a voice so quiet Buddy had to lean forward to hear him.

"I'm talking about Joey making a deal for himself. And, you know he's going to hang it on someone else. And, I think you know who it's going to be."

"Not me, not me. I'm not taking the heat for this, oh man. He can't pin this on me. I was only following orders. You gotta believe me man, I didn't do nothing."

"Why don't you tell me all about it, Buddy?" Alan prompted.

"Okay, but you gotta cut me a deal," he whined, shaking a little less than before.

"Let's start at the beginning, Bud. Who was in charge?" Alan knew the interview was being videotaped and he wanted everything nice and clear.

"Enis and Joey come to us. They say they heard that Bobby Pearl's gang was planning to hit the store. Somebody in Bobby's gang snitched to Joey. Well, Joey said he had a plan to outfox Bobby's hit. He put together this job real fast. We were goin' to be in the store before his guys got there and we would overtake them, tie them up, and leave them for the cops to grab. Meanwhile we would do the job and grab all the money."

"So what went wrong?"

"Well, Bobby and his pals put up a fight. We knew they would, but Joey figured we could take them easy, only one of the guys took a knife to the gut and started to scream. There was blood all over the place and Joey panicked. I don't think he was prepared for them to fight like they did. I don't know who knifed Sid. It could have been maybe Joey, Bobby, or anybody. Anyhow, we got the hell out of there as fast as we could. I don't know anything else, I swear it." he looked relieved to have gotten all that out and slumped back in his chair.

"I want you to take this pad and write out everything you just told me and then sign it," Alan instructed him as he slid the pad and a pen across the table to him.

"Do it now and I'll be back when you're finished, we'll talk more then."

"Okay, then we got a deal?" Buddy asked with a trace of hope in his voice.

Chapter Forty-Six

Ralph and Alan sat together in the small office that housed the fingerprint section. Alan twirled the inker in his hand while Ralph wiped the desk with the paper toweling that was provided to the people who have their prints taken.

Alan looked at his partner and saw he was deep in his own thoughts. He coughed into his hand, his eyes searching Ralph's face for a hint as to what he was thinking.

"Huh, what?" Ralph asked, his eyes focusing slowly on Alan.

"Ralph, you haven't said a word for almost 10 minutes, I know the information we got from these guys hasn't been corroborated, but I think Buddy's story holds water. The rivalry between the gangs could explain the mess at the store. We still don't know who's responsible for the murder of the creep in the back, but we're getting close."

"Yes, but I'm still fixated on this guy Lew Wallace. The story he tells is kind of hinky. Everybody we talk to gives him kudos for being the one they could count on in any situation. Maybe he's too good to be true, but, on the other hand, he shows up at the nick of time, always. How does he manage that? How does he happen to be the one who bails all these people out? Could he be our vigilante?"

"You've got a lot on your mind pal, this guy Lew does seem too good to be true, but no one says anything negative about him. I went back through his childhood history. There were stories about him even then, but they were all on the good side. Helping people even at an early age is all they say about him. No, I can't see him doing anything violent. He's too much of a nice guy."

"Okay Al, getting back to the bikers, what I think we should do is to go over to the hospital and get this guy Bobby Pearl on record. I want to charge him with anything we can come up with, attempted burglary, murder, and rape, whatever. We have to make something stick so that we have some leverage."

"So, let's go," Alan said, as he thrust himself out of the metal torture chair he had been saddled with.

"Right, but before we go let's make sure he's still there. These characters don't always follow the rules or doctors' orders."

"Okay, I'll call the hospital."

"While you're doing that I'm going to get together with the Chief of Police. Joey Peanuts and Buddy should be kept in different cells far away from each other. I don't know if he knows to keep them separated, we don't want Joey to know about Buddy's statement, yet."

Alan went to call the hospital and Ralph went to talk to the Chief.

Chapter Forty-Seven

Lew, in the meantime, had his hands full trying to get the store ready for business. There was yellow crime scene tape all over the store and he had to work around it. Grey fingerprint dust covered a great deal of the equipment in the back of the store. The police had left one uniformed officer to oversee the wreckage and to make sure none of the areas were disturbed.

Lew was sifting through the debris, attempting to put things in order when his hand closed around an object that was foreign to the part of the store, and as he lifted it out, he was surprised to see a long stain encrusted switchblade.

"Hmm," he wondered, "I wonder how long this has been laying here. A long time?" he thought to himself as he slipped it into his pocket and almost immediately forgot about it.

He worked the entire day without giving it a second thought until his wife Linda discovered it later that evening as she was emptying his pockets.

"Lew, what is this thing?"

"Oh that, I don't know."

"You don't know?"

"I'm afraid to say I haven't the vaguest idea. I must have found it in the store."

The conversation went on for a little while as the knife sat on a counter, giving Lew's wife an odd feeling, which Lew could not explain.

They were at odds as to what to do with it. Either they could forget about it or turn it over to the police, whatever they did would impact their lives from that moment on.

They left the problem sitting there on the counter while they slept on it overnight.

In the morning, the problem remained and they still had not come to a conclusion.

Chapter Forty-Eight

"Chief Lewis, we need to sit down with you and have a clarifying chat with you," Ralph said, with Alan right behind him.

"Sure, come on in boys, grab a seat. What do you need?"

"I wanted to make sure you had enough cells here to keep those bikers separated. It wouldn't do to have them get together and coordinate their stories."

"Oh, I agree with you, and I did segregate them. It's the normal thing to do here, although we don't usually have so many suspects at one time."

"I suspected so, and I hope this is the worst you ever see. Where I come from, the district I mean, we see all too much of it."

"I can imagine. But, you know that this is not my first job in law enforcement. I came from the Detroit PD a few years ago."

"No, I didn't know that."

"Yes, well we saw our share out there, so I know the routine well enough."

Chief Lewis was a big husky man. He stood about 6'3" tall and weighed in at 225 lbs. His hands were the size of catcher's mitts and his shoulders were as wide as the doorframe. In other words, he was a handful and not one given to backing down to bikers.

"Okay, Chief. Thanks for everything", Ralph said as he and Alan prepared to leave when Lewis said, "I hope you don't think Lew Wallace has anything to do with this, do you?"

Ralph turned back and looked at the Chief directly in his eyes, his mind trying to process the question.

"I really don't know, but his name keeps coming up every time I turn around. It gives me pause and I don't really know how to wrap my mind around it yet. I hope he doesn't have anything to do with it, I really do."

Chief Lewis went on to say, "Well I think you'll find he doesn't. He's one of the good guys."

"Okay, Chief, I'll keep that in mind", Ralph said as he left the office, thinking about Lew again.

Chapter Forty-Nine

"Hey, who's in charge here?" roared one-half of the most unlikely couples ever to don biker leathers. "I said 'who the hell is in charge here?'"

The voice echoed off the walls of the police station, windows seemed to rattle in their frames, and all eyes were riveted on the sight of the sound.

Appearing before the Sgt. at the front desk was a pair of the oddest people ever seen at the station.

At 5'3" and 190 lbs., a rather short rotund gnome of a man that appeared to be a biker. He was filthy at every exposed part of his strange body. He had a magnificently unkempt flowing red beard and a ragged drooping moustache. Hair emanated from each nostril and he was a bald as the proverbial cue ball, and was quite filthy up there. The stench that encompassed his very being was almost equal to a garbage dump, but the dump came in second to him.

The only thing sure about him was his voice was as strident as was his smell.

Following behind him was the second oddest thing to enter the station house. What appeared to be a woman who stood 6' tall and 125 lbs., as thin as a rail with glowing red hair, cut in the newest fashion. The only thing that connected them was the fact that she too reeked of garbage, which was fortunate for her as she had the dubious distinction of riding behind him on his tricked out chopper of a bike. Her exposed skin was also as filthy as his was, so as a couple they seemingly fit.

Once again he roared, "I said, 'who the hell is in charge here?'"

Sergeant Kelly, the officer in charge of the desk grimaced at the stench and the roar from the little man in front of him.

"Excuse me, sir," Sgt Kelly said a bit sarcastically "What can I do for you?"

"My name is Edgar Allen Poe, and no smart remarks from you or anyone else," he said in a slightly lower but still a loud voice.

"They call me the Poet, as you can easily discern from my name", he intoned.

"Okay, Mr. Poe," Sgt Kelly snickered "What can the Arthur Police Department do for you?"

"I want to know who is in charge here, and I know it isn't you Sergeant. So point me in the correct direction and I'll be out of your hair."

"As pleasant as that would be, can I possibly know what you have in mind? Why do you need to see the person in charge?"

"That's for the person in charge to know, and you…have no need to know."

"I'm sorry, Mr. Poe. But, that's exactly wrong. If you want to see someone, I'm the one you have to tell. And, if I'm not entirely mistaken, you already know that. So…I will ask you again Mr. Poe, just what is your business here?"

With a look of exasperation, Poe took in the Sgt's stern look, puffed his round whisker-covered cheeks, and blew out a rather foul odor of feral food that had probably rotted in his unpolished teeth, of which he had only a few left.

"Okay, have it your way, officer. I'm a member of the Cross Social Club. As you can readily see by the back of my jacket", he turned and beneath a layer of filth, a silver cross did indeed show up.

"So, what do you want?" demanded Kelly.

"Gawdammit" Poe roared again, "I thought I told you so many times, I want to see the man in charge."

"I'm going to tell you one more time before I get someone here to escort you out of the building, you cannot raise your voice and if you do again I will do exactly that. Now-very-quietly- what-do-you-want?" Kelly slowly spoke out.

Quieter than ever, Poe said, "I have information about the killing of one of my brothers and the break in at the sports store. Now, can you help me, please?"

"That's better, if you will just wait over there by the bench, I'll call and get someone who can help you", Kelly pointed to the furthest point in the room, relieved to have the stench from both of them far away from him.

The strange duo marched to the bench where the woman delicately placed herself down while Poe started to pace back and forth.

"Phew," the patrolman sitting next to Kelly said, "What a pair, boy do they stink."

"Yeah, I think they bathe in the dumps outside of town, if they bathe at all. Which I doubt," Kelly said as he put a dab of Vicks up his nose and handed the jar to the other officer, "Here this'll help".

"Thanks, Sarge", he said as he applied it to his nose, also. "I've got to carry this stuff myself."

Kelly punched the Chief's number into the phone, "Chief," he said, "You wouldn't believe what I have down here demanding to see you or someone in charge. I don't think you would want them to come up to your office. If you came down here you'll understand why."

"Okay, Kelly. I'll be right down."

Chapter Fifty

"Okay, Mr. Poe," Chief Lewis said, affording the filthy biker and his lady friend the courtesy of a seat in his office, thinking to himself that they will probably have to fumigate not only his office but the front desk area as well.

"What is it that you had to disrupt my entire department with your, and I don't mind saying, very loud and bombastic voice. And please keep it down to a quieter volume."

"In deference to your hospitality, I shall endeavor to do as you have requested. As to why I am here sir, I have the need to clarify some misconceptions your department is under."

"And what misconceptions would that be?"

"The fact that you think the someone who perpetrated the demise of my fellow motorcyclist companion is one of us, the Cross I mean."

"And who may I surmise that person would be, may I ask?"

"Why, Chief, I think it would be obvious as to whom that unfortunate person would be.

"Why don't you enlighten me," the Chief said as his nose crinkled at the odor of Poe's body that invaded every corner of his office.

"I will certainly do that, but first you have to afford me and my lady some sort of protection."

"Do you think you're in some sort of danger? I would think that you could take care of yourselves in any situation. I mean it appears you have been in the life for a good while", Lewis said.

"Yes, you would think so, but unfortunately situations change. And, a person of my stature, I know you won't agree, is not a formidable figure despite my obvious intelligence. The only large part of my countenance is my voice and my vocabulary, which doesn't present a defense against the ones who really know me. I, or we, have kept somewhat under the radar most of the time and unfortunately we are treated as a joke to many."

"I think I can see that."

"So, when I tell you what I know, our very personage will require more than a modicum of safety."

"Mr. Poe, I have to hear exactly what you are referring to before I make any commitments. I'm sure you can understand that."

"Um, yes, I can, but can you assure us that if our information is helpful you are in a position to provide what we require?" Poe said leaning forward towards Lewis's body.

Chief Lewis said, stifling a gag response, "If I can't satisfy your requirement I have detectives from the NYPD who can, if your information is valid."

Every time Poe or his lady friend moved, the odor from their bodies exploded in puffs of indescribable aromas, causing an invisible cloud to encompass the entire room.

"Chief, we appreciate your discretion in this matter and I can tell you that the perpetrator of this homicide is now incarcerated in the Arthur Hospital with a rather delicate injury to his person."

"Are you referring to Bobby Pearl?"

"Exactly."

"And how do you know this?"

"First hand, I was privy to the merchandise of the proposed burglary. Being that my presence was not solicited and being that no one pays much attention to me, I found it rather easy to trail along, unseen by my compatriots of the Cross and observe every instance of the incident."

"And?"

"And while three of the Cross' club members ransacked the interior, I also observed the aforementioned Pearl and four of his club members slip through the front door."

"So?"

"So, I observed from my vantage point Bobby Pearl encountering the deceased, only he was discovered after Bobby walked away from him. It was then that I also observed the blood emanating from his nether regions, his belly, so to speak."

"So, it's your contention that Bobby Pearl killed this person and that you witnessed the entire, and I repeat the entire procedure. Do I have that correct?"

"Yes."

"But tell me, Mr. Poe, you said the person who was done in is not one of the Cross."

"Did I say that?"

"Yes, you did, so my question to you is, what motive would Bobby Pearl have to do what you are accusing him of? Why would he do that?"

"I don't have that answer, sir. But I did observe what I observed."

"In that case, the only thing I can do is issue an order to arrest Mr. Pearl, based on your eyewitness account. But, you also realize that I have to pursue an arrest of anyone who was at the scene. And may I point out, Mr. Poe, that you fall into that category, according to what you have told me here", Chief Lewis stated emphatically.

"But, but, sir, I have done you a public service, you can't be serious sir!!!" Poe argued equally emphatically.

"Ah, but I am. You have just implicated yourself Mr. Poe, you have just placed yourself at the scene of the crime, and that my smelly friend means that you are under arrest. Officer Tornillo, please come in here and place Mr. Poe in custody and throw his stinky ass in a cell."

"But, but you can't do this, you can't do this", Poe repeated as Tornillo placed his handcuffs on him, albeit from a distance, as the stench still emanated strongly, and led him away.

Chapter Fifty-One

Ralph and Alan were informed of Poe's arrest and with the account of his statements from the Chief. They proceeded to the hospital to get Bobby Pearl.

"Ralph, do you think this Poe character's accusation is really true? I mean, couldn't it be just revenge that the Cross would send a fall guy, a goat, to walk into the station and without a second thought open himself up to an obvious arrest. I mean, this guy, if we are led to believe is supposed to be more or less intelligent."

"I think that no matter how intelligent this guy might be, he was sent to throw a potential enemy to the cops, in hopes that the thing at the store would stop with Bobby's arrest and it would take the heat off the Cross. I think Joey Peanuts is not the brain he thinks he is and now that it's backfired on him, he might regret it. The guy is definitely an asshole!!!"

"But now, both camps are on the hook and we have probable cause to haul all of them in. Only where can we put them all? The town's jail isn't large enough to house the whole bunch of them."

"Yes, I know. But, we can ask Manhattan for help? You might have forgotten that this is still their jurisdiction and they have the responsibility to back us up."

"You're right, Ralph. I forget about that in all the confusion. You know being here, you lose track of where you are. This is like being out west somewhere. It's like being in the Wild West all over again. Do you know what I mean?"

"Yeah, this small town stuff gets under your skin after a while. But, we're big city cops and we can't forget it. If we fall into small town traps we can overlook certain things, like there's a vigilante on the loose here."

"Right, Ralph, but we still can't pin that on anyone yet."

"Our only suspect so far is Lew Wallace, although he is such an unlikely suspect that it's such a stretch that I'm disinclined to believe it, but no one else fills the bill, so far."

"Maybe we have to take another run at him. What do you think?"

"Aahh, I don't know, maybe. Let's see what turns up."

"Ralph", Chief Lewis strode into their makeshift office, "What do you think we should do with this skank Poe? I don't know if I buy what he's putting out about this killing. Maybe you guys should take a shot at him."

"He claims he saw the killing first hand?"

That's what he said, but he's such a sleaze that, well, I don't know. But before you go in there I have to warn you…he stinks to high heaven…"

"What do you mean, he stinks?"

"Just what I said, this man, or whatever you want to call him, smells like the worst garbage I've ever smelled. Trust me. I've smelled some pretty rotten stuff. But this guy beats it all."

"I know his name is Poe. What is his full name?"

"Oh, you're not going to believe this one. He claims it is Edgar Allan Poe. That's right. You heard it, Edgar Allan Poe."

"You're joking, aren't you, Chief?"

"Nope, and his girlfriend's name is, and it's a good thing you're both sitting down, is Lorelie Lee."

"Stink or not, I gotta see this," Ralph nodded to Alan and got up and all three practically trotted out of the office.

Chapter Fifty-Two

The fog was not as thick and cloying as others had been in the past but it didn't seem to matter to Lew. He wandered through it uncaring of where he was heading. He only knew that he was moving in a sort of gliding motion.

The fact was that he had been, in actuality, in this fog state for more than two days, and he had been traveling in a northern route out of town, out of the outskirts, into another township, and then further on did not faze him.

He only knew he felt an abounding feeling of peace, the troubles of the past few days faded as he went further into the fog.

No one who knew him would be surprised that they had not seen him for a couple of days. They understood that Lew had gone missing so many times and had eventually returned as if nothing had ever happened to him in a negative way.

Ralph and Alan, who did not know Lew as the others did, only knew that a person of interest was missing. Their concern was more about the enmity the bikers had shown towards him, and they feared harm had come to him because of that.

Lew's wife Linda did not appear overly concerned when Ralph and Alan called and questioned about his whereabouts.

"Mrs. Wallace," Ralph asked, "is there any one place he would go? Any place he has gone before? I'm only asking because we don't want anything to happen to him, physically I mean."

She simply said, "Detective, I have never asked him where he goes. I don't think he even knows when he is in a particular state, which I think he is in now. So I can't answer your question, sorry."

Ralph looked at Alan with a wry smile on his face, he said, "Boy, this guy has it made, his wife knows nothing about his comings and goings and nobody seem to be concerned about them. He could have another complete life elsewhere and nobody even cares. Wow, what a guy, don't you envy him? I mean…wow…"

"No, I don't envy him, Ralph. Think about it. He's off somewhere, no one knows where. What if he's in danger, no one knows if he'll ever come back. Forget about the fact that he always seems to come back. What if someone has gotten to him, and he's laying somewhere needing help or already dead? Envy him? No way, pal."

"I see your point, Al. But then again what if he's shacked up with someone? His other family, who when he leaves them to come back here, doesn't worry either. I couldn't do that, you know, if I was married. But then again we don't know what he's doing or where the hell he is. Alan we've got to find him."

"Right, but where do we look?"

"Well, he doesn't own a car, so he's either on foot or he took a bus, so we check the bus station and have the Chief send some cars out to scour the countryside. He's got to be somewhere."

"I'll get to the Chief and Al you check the bus station."

As they split up to do their assigned chores Lew was about one hundred miles away at this point, still enfolded in the soft peaceful fog.

Chapter Fifty-Three

The nurses assigned to Bobby Pearl were all in a twitter, they had never cared for someone like him. His body was covered by a multitude of tattoos of every imaginable scene. His arms were a tangle of vines with snakes of different colors entwined within them. His back sported a huge battleship with its guns exploding with white clouds from which large shells pushed through. Sea battles of every kind surrounded the large ship. His chest and stomach was a cacophony of color, with flowers and a dozen different hearts with arrows piercing and blood dripping among the various names on each heart. His legs front and back, were equally festooned with an abundance of lightning bolts and storm clouds with raindrops covering every inch of leg, from thighs to ankles.

The nurses treated him like a celebrity, they had no idea he was an active rapist and womanizer of helpless young girls, besides being a convicted felon who had evaded the most evil of crimes such as murder...so far.

In their naiveté, they believed him to be a romantic figure, but then they had no basis for comparison.

They did not recognize the look in his eyes whenever one of the young nurses passed close to him. They failed to see the lust, the absolute raw evil that came over and clouded the blue of his eyes with a hint of red, menacing the rims.

Bobby enjoyed the virtual freedom of the hospital room. He, aside from the pain between his legs, reveled in the attention he was getting from the female staff. The prospect of not having a penis rarely entered his thoughts. As far as he was concerned, he was still the man he was before the incident. As the narcissist he had always been, he believed that when a nurse changed his crotch dressing they were admiring his manhood. Little did he realize they were pitying him his missing part, but that was his ego's way of dealing with his problem.

Chapter Fifty-Four

Slowly the fog dissipated, the town seemed different somehow. The streets were not where he remembered them to be. The shops were foreign to him and as his eyes grew accustomed to the sights, Lew came to the realization that this was not Arthur.

"Hmm, I wonder where I am?" he mumbled to himself, "How did I get here, and how long have I been away from home?"

People passed him on the street, they did not look familiar, and they did not give him a second look.

He looked for something, anything that would give him a clue as to what town he was in, and he hoped he had not done anything remotely bad that could have made it necessary for him to leave his hometown.

The only thing he did know was that he missed his wife and the life to which he belonged. There was nothing more that he wanted than to be back in his home.

It had been two weeks since he walked into the fog, but to Lew it had only seemed to be mere seconds. Much had happened in the town of Arthur that he was unaware of, and that Lew had set in motion by leaving.

He wandered into a drug store and approached the counter where a woman stood behind the cash register.

"Excuse me Miss, could you tell me where I am?"

"Of course," she replied, "You're in Walgreens."

"No, I'm sorry, I knew that. But what town is this?"

"Oh, I'm sorry, yes, you're in Kingston," she said looking at him with an open smile.

"Kingston, please forgive me, miss. But where is Kingston?"

"Well," she started to get a little frustrated but her smile remained and she remained calm when she answered, "Kingston is in New Jersey, and that is in the United States, of America, of course," she said as if he was an alien.

"Kingston, New Jersey, would you happen to know how far Arthur is from here," he asked.

"I don't know your friend Arthur, but you could look in the phone book. Maybe you can find his address in there," she said a little testily.

"No, no, you don't understand. I'm sorry I'm being such a pest, but Arthur is the town I live in, not a person. Although I'm sure there is a person somewhere named Arthur," he said with a little laugh in his voice.

"Oh, I'm sorry, I really didn't understand you. So you are lost are you?"

"I guess I don't know how I got here and I don't know how to get back home. I'm sorry to have bothered you. I do thank you for the time you have given me."

"Well, why don't you go to the police station down the street, they will probably be able to help you there", she said.

"Thank you, I will. And thank you for your kindness", Lew said with an earnest smile on his face as he turned to go.

As Lew exited the drug store, the fog enshrouded him once more. He smiled again, as if being embraced by an old friend. Kingston, New Jersey was now a forgotten memory.

Chapter Fifty-Five

The stench hung over the entire interrogation room like a moldy blanket. It clung to the stark grey walls, the cold metal table, and most of all the, Poet, Edgar Allan Poe and his erstwhile female companion Lorelie Lee, as he liked to call her.

Her real name was Gladys Murray, but she pushed that mundane name so far back in her memory she never thought of herself as Gladys anymore.

Ralph had not wanted to subject Alan to the atmosphere in the room and said he would continue the questioning by Officer Nicholas Bell and himself. Bell was not overjoyed to be in the room. But, he would not complain as he believed he could learn something from the New York detective, so he kept to his own thoughts.

"Okay Mr. Poe, you know who I am, but in case you have forgotten. I'm Detective Ralph Bloom of the NYPD."

Poe cleared his throat with a sickly cough and looked at Ralph with slanted eyes. He said with a wrinkle of his nose, as if he smelled something unfamiliar to him, "Are you a Jew?"

"What? What the hell are you talking about man? Are you crazy or are you trying to get me to paste you one in that foul thing you call a mouth? Maybe you forget where you are, pal…but I do the asking here and you provide the answers. You answer my questions or, by gawd, you will not see the sun for a good long time. Do you understand?" Ralph fumed.

"Hey, take it easy man. I just asked an innocent question. No need to explode, boy, you sure are on edge," Poe said as he held his hands in front of him in a defensive pose.

"Listen, MR. Poe," Ralph stressed the mister part, "I want some answers, and I want them now!!! What you told Chief Lewis, I want you to repeat the entire statement again and don't leave anything out. Get it!!!"

"Okay, I get it," Poe said and went to recount everything he had reported to the Chief, as Ralph consulted the written statement that Poe had signed.

When he had finished, Ralph looked at him and said, "Thank you and now you are under arrest for complicity to commit a crime and for withholding evidence in a homicide."

"Officer, please place this man," Ralph said with a sneer "Under arrest and escort him to a holding cell. Make sure he is nowhere near anyone else. We don't want his stinky self-subjected to anyone else."

"Yes sir, Detective. Mr. Poe, please stand up and place your hands behind your back," Officer Bell said as he held his breath and placed hand cuffs on Poe's filthy hands, standing as far from Poe as he possibly could and effectively accomplish his job.

"But I cooperated. How can you do this to me? I protest this treatment."

"Too bad, Poe. You made your bed and now you've got to lay in it," Ralph said in a monotone voice "Please, Officer, take him away before I vomit."

Poe loudly railed at everyone as he was led away.

Ralph looked at Lorelie Lee and said, "I strongly suggest you find someone else to hook up with, but maybe you should stay away from bikers. Oh, and another suggestion…Take-A-Bath."

Chapter Fifty-Six

Lew's fog trip took him far away from New Jersey. In his fugue state, he had no idea that his trip this time took him in a southwesterly direction. Through small towns and through large cities he went. He stopped for what seemed like minutes in some locations but not long enough to establish where he was before the fog enshrouded him again. It took no toll on his physical being, but his mind attempted to evaluate his situation, but to no avail.

He could not comprehend the fog's motive for taking him so far away nor could he do anything to compensate for them. He just seemed to wander, unseen by anyone. And, but for the occasional stop, he saw no one.

Again and again, he would pass over uninhabited fields and at times through places crowded with people and all kinds of humanity, but no one intended for him...until.

A huge billboard said 'Welcome to Dream City, the most progressive city in the West' off to the right side of the road. "Dream City, three miles ahead" was the directions at the bottom of the sign.

Lew stood stock still, his eyes scanned to the right and then to the left... nothing... His head swiveled to the rear, still…nothing…just the sign.

He also noticed that there was no fog. The road dust filled his nostrils and stung his eyes. He did not feel tired nor did he question how he had arrived at this desolate place.

He shrugged his shoulders and strode on. Starting this new journey towards Dream City, hoping that he could at last land somewhere that would make some sense to him.

The three-mile walk was pleasant enough, no one passed him on the road, no person, no cars, no animals, nothing. The sun was high and very pleasantly warm against his face and the walk was easy.

Eventually he reached the edge of the so-called city. So far, all he saw was another sign, brand new stating, "You are now entering Dream City, Welcome. Population building, But not yet done" no evidence of a city appeared in front of Lew.

Lew scratched his head, wondering where Dream City could possibly be. He picked up his pace and literally strode boldly into an area where there was an enormous hole in the middle of the road.

"What the?" he thought, "What have I stumbled into here? Why have I been brought here to a hole in the ground? What kind of joke is this?"

Chapter Fifty-Seven

Linda Wallace hesitated before walking through the doors of the police station. She had second thoughts about what she was about to do, but she could see no other way. It had been five days since she had last seen Lew. Although in her heart she knew he had not fallen ill or had been in an accident, she was still concerned.

In the past, Lew had not come home for a night and even on one occasion a full day, but something about this five-day missing act was strange to her.

She approached the officer at the front desk, looked up at a youngish face, full of innocence, and said, "Excuse me".

The young officer, Patrolman Simmons, looked down and saw a woman who although appearing calm, he noticed a strain to her voice.

"Yes, ma'am. Can I help you?"

"I think I need to see someone about my husband, he seems to be missing."

"May I have your name please?"

"Linda Wallace, my husband is Lew Wallace and I haven't seen him for five days. I need someone to help me find him," she said in a slightly shaky voice.

"Okay, Mrs. Wallace. I'll get someone down here. Won't you have a seat?" he pointed to the bench by the wall.

"Thank you, young man" Linda said and sat down primly on the cold metal bench."

"It will only be a minute," Simmons said.

As she sat, she looked around and spied the wanted posters affixed to a bulletin board. All sorts of dangerous faces looked out at the large room with their crimes and vital statistics imprinted alongside each face.

She shuddered and hoped her dear husband had not run into anyone on these posters. She thought to herself, "Heaven forbid he should run into any of those".

The elevator across from her opened and another officer, Sam Urban stepped out and ambled across to her. "Mrs. Wallace?" he inquired.

She looked up at him and said, "Yes".

"I'm Sam Urban. I'll take you up to the detectives on the case. Please follow me, if you would."

"Of course," she said as she rose and shook his outstretched hand.

He stepped aside to allow her to enter the elevator and pressed the button for the third floor.

They rode in silence to the third floor. She looked at the floor until the door opened and Urban preceded her. He led her to one of the desks in the middle of the room.

Fax machines fed reams of paper out of their openings, phones rang at other desks. She observed a small kitchen area where a coffee machine was brewing a pot of coffee and a half open Dunkin Donuts box sat pushed to one side.

The desk she sat at was devoid of paper work except for one manila folder in front of the empty chair across from of her.

Alan Beckman turned a corner and approached the desk where he stopped and introduced himself, "Mrs. Wallace, I'm Detective Beckman. We met at your house a few days ago, I hope you remember me?"

"Of course I do, Detective. I'm glad it's you and not some stranger. My husband Lew is missing and I need your help," she said with tears forming at the side of her eyes.

"What do you mean he's missing?"

"I mean I have not seen him for the last five days and I'm very nervous. He's never, ever been gone for more than one night or one day and I'm worried sick something has happened to him."

"I can understand your concern, he hasn't called or anything?" Alan asked looking deeply into her amber eyes.

"No calls, no anything, Detective. I'm really worried, what with the things that have been happening around here lately. He did bring the knife in here didn't he? He said he was going to."

"Yes, as a matter of fact he did. That was, let me see, six days ago and we spoke to him at length. We didn't see any reason to suspect anything to connect him with it, but it was used in a crime. We saw no reason to hold him and he left."

"Oh, my gawd. I told him it was a bad thing, that knife. I told him."

"Yes," Alan said, "Anyway, we will put out an all-points bulletin and we won't stop until we find him. I personally don't think he's come to any harm. But, I assure you, we won't stop."

"Please, Detective, find him. I'm so worried."

"We'll do our very best, Mrs. Wallace. I promise you."

"Thank you, and do you mind if I wait here. I have no one to go home to right now," she said with a plaintive cry in her voice.

"We don't mind. There's a lounge area downstairs that you might find more comfortable."

"Thank you again, Detective. I'll wait down there," she said as Alan got the elevator for her and waited until she disappeared before going back to his desk with a heavy sigh.

Chapter Fifty-Eight

Meanwhile, Bobby Pearl was captivating a cute nurse with tales of his adventures, some of which were mere fabrications tailored to enhance his rather mundane past. He constructed some of the most bizarre circumstances that had the little nurse's eyes wide-open in amazement. Tales of his daring-do rolled off his tongue as easily as butter melting in a hot frying pan.

Little did she know that Pearl was a known bully and gang rapist, who had perpetrated the most evil crimes that the city of Arthur had ever seen. The murder of one of the rival gang's members still hung over his head as a person of extreme interest, but that was lost on the little nurse.

"And you wouldn't believe it Nurse Mary", Bobby said with such an innocent look on his face. "The mayor gave me the key to the city for my many services to the citizens and donated a plaque honoring me, can you believe it?" He went on charming nurse Mary with an evil glint in his eye.

His motives were evident, to get the young nurse in his clutches and to hell with the consequences, and it appeared to be working.

"Bobby," Nurse Mary said plaintively, "Do you think the police will be prosecuting you for anything? I mean, do you think you'll be leaving the hospital anytime soon?"

"Oh, don't you worry your pretty little head about anything Mary. I'll be around for a long time and you're not getting rid of me so fast. I have big plans for you and me, believe me, kid."

She practically melted on the spot and looked so adoringly at Bobby that he almost broke into loud laughter at the ease at which he had suckered her in.

"Mary, do you think you can get me some pain pills? My crotch hurts so much now."

Right then Bobby came to the full realization that no matter what heinous plans he had for Nurse Mary, he had no way to get the job done…he had no penis. "I have no penis…damn it. How could I forget so soon?" he asked himself as she went off to get him some medication. "Oh well, sucking her in was fun for a while," he grimaced to himself.

Chapter Fifty-Nine

Lew stood virtually dead center in the Dream City proposed site. Nothing moved, birds roosted on mounds of earth that had been dug up by some invisible earthmover that was nowhere in sight. White clouds dotted the sky and the sun was high overhead and cast a calming effect on him.

He scanned 360 degrees without turning his body, only swiveling his head. Something was buzzing in the back of his mind, something that was tantalizing him but he could not successfully bring it forth.

Sounds, like voices, rebounded in the deep cortex of his brain. They did not seem to be connected to any one idea.

The utter silence was in one way disturbing and in another sense, it was quite peaceful, his feelings were wavering between the two.

It was then he saw in the far distance, past where he passed the sign, a figure that shimmered in the intense sunlight, somewhat like a dream figure that grew larger as it passed the sign.

All in white, it appeared to float above the road. Wisps of light surrounded it and the closer it came Lew recognized it as a human, although he could not see clearly if it was male or female. Closer and closer, it came. And, when it was about 20 feet from Lew, he heard the voice, low and rumbling. It became more distinct and he discerned that it was addressing him, using his name.

"Lew Wallace," it said as it stopped almost ten feet from him, "Lew Wallace" it repeated, "I'm glad you have finally found us."

"Who, who are you? And how do you know my name?"

"I, excuse me, we are your conscience, and we know all about you, of course."

"We? Do you mean my conscience is more than one?"

"Yes, of course. Everyone's conscience is a diverse thing, only people cannot conceive of it."

"I guess I can understand that, I guess. But why have you made me come here?" he fluttered his hand in a motion that encompassed Dream City.

"This is the only place in your mind that we could reveal ourselves to you, where you would be fully receptive to what we must make you believe."

"Believe what?"

"Believe that you have a gift, one that helps you to know that you are a good soul, and the fogs you experience are only in your mind. But in your case, the fog protects you from harm."

"Okay," Lew said slowly as a troubling thought entered his head "But why take me this far from home, couldn't you tell me this before and closer to home?"

"No, Lew. We had to remove you from the pressures you were putting on yourself, so you would be completely receptive."

"Receptive to what?"

"Receptive to the fact that you are not guilty of any wrongdoing, that the knife that turned up has nothing to do with all the mayhem back home."

"So, now that I know this, what am I expected to do about it all of this?"

"That is for you to decide. As your conscience, we can only place the thoughts in your head. You need to come to the conclusion. You will do the right thing, it may take you a while, but we feel you will take the right road."

"But I have been away such a long time, how can I make a decision when my entire life I have been doing things that I don't believe were what I have wanted to do. Has all this been your doing? And, if it is…why? Why me? Is this supposed to be a punishment for me doing something wrong? Or, a blessing? I don't know anymore."

"Lew, it isn't a punishment for anything you have done or will do. It is the very way of things, but you have done the things that are right. All the fogs you have been subjected to are what we, your conscience have led you to and you have equipped yourself admirably. And, to tell you the truth, I take all the credit for it."

"Well," Lew said in disbelief "I wish now your influence could lead me to the right decision about what's happened in Arthur, believe me."

"Lew," the voice said, "No matter what happens you will make the right decision, and you can believe me, I make all your decisions, meaning you."

At that, the voice faded and the fog rolled in again. Lew looked around and Dream City faded from view.

Chapter Sixty

Joey Peanuts, Edgar Allen Poe--the Poet, and all the members of the Cross Motorcycle Club were being interviewed by the detectives on a daily basis. So far, the only thing they could be charged with was the major crime of burglary of an establishment.

Some of the members directly involved pleaded innocent of the crime. They pled that they were not directly involved, but the truth of the matter was that they knew of the intent and therefore were complicit, even if they were not there.

Ralph and Alan had their hands full, half of their charges were bikers with former criminal records with warrants out for their capture, and many others were candidates for future incarceration. Ninety percent of them were grease covered and smelled as if soap and water were a distant memory or a dirty word. The uniform of the club consisted of various combinations of denim, leather and rags, with jewelry ranging from body piercing, earrings, nose and tongue clips, chains of all dimensions, and spiked bracelets of all sizes and shapes.

Before being interviewed and or jailed, these objects had to be collected, tagged and placed in a secure location, a lockbox on wheels had to be constructed, as all the metal weighed a couple of hundred pounds that no mere cardboard box was sufficient to safely hold.

"Ralph," Alan asked with a whimsical look on his face, "Could we melt all this down" pointing to the mass of metal. "And forge enough handcuffs to handle all these guys?"

Laughing loudly, Ralph replied, "I think we should melt it down and build a new jail to house them all".

"Maybe we should invest it in shower facilities. They sure could use them, but I don't think they would even recognize a shower if it splashed in their faces. Man, did you ever smell a group like this before, phew…" Alan said as he held his nose.

"Did you ever see a sight like this Poet and his gal pal?" Alan said, "How would you like to be locked in a small room with those two?"

"I don't even like to be in the same town, much less a room with them," Ralph answered, "That's a 10-4, buddy."

Chapter Sixty-One

"I think something should be done to put the Pearl out of his misery. He will never be the same, Bobby. And, we need to help him over the de-penis-sizing. What do you think?" Bernie Tampon said to a shadow in the corner.

"What do I think? What do you think I think?" the shadow said. "You call me here and propose to put him down and you ask what I think?"

"Yeah, what do you think", Bernie asked again.

"Well, I think you got an idea that someone, anyone but you, should do the job. That's what I think."

"That's why I asked you here, man. Somebody, and I'll never tell, should do it. And, I believe you know just the someone to do it. Am I right?"

"Yeah, you're right. I do know the perfect person to get this done, but what's in it for me? Let me get this straight, Tampon. I never do anything for nothing. And, if I get this done for you, you owe me big time. Get it?" the shadow emphasized this statement with a hard poke into Bernie's chest, Hard enough that Bernie winced with a sharp gasp.

"Yeah, man. You don't have to get rough. I dig, and I'm not going to screw you. Trust me, I got something big for you," Bernie said rubbing the spot where the shadow had almost pierced the skin.

"Trust you, Bernie? I trust you as far as I can throw this building. So don't give me that crap, 'trust me' crap. I need to see something concrete, like up front. Do you dig that Bernie?"

"Okay, okay. Don't get bent out of shape here," Bernie said as he reached behind him and came up with a leather pouch that was fat with something stuffed inside.

"This is just a down payment you understand, but you can't tell anyone or show it around."

"Let's just see what you consider just a down payment, pal. After that we can talk, if I decide it's enough to interest me."

"It's enough, it's enough, trust me."

"Ha, there you go with that trust me $#!+. I told you how much I trust you, Bernie," the shadow still didn't come into the light, but his heavily tattooed hand grabbed the pouch and pulled it back, opening it just a little.

"Well now. This looks like a pretty good start, Bern. I think I can help you with your little problem. I'll need a day or two to get everything in place." He stood and it seemed like Bernie was dwarfed by the shadow's size. He still stayed in the darkness while he strode purposely out of the bar, the door closing silently behind him.

"Whew", Bernie breathed a sigh of relief as the shadow's back passed through the door. "I'm glad that's over," he said to himself. "I don't like that guy at all, but that should take care of the Pearl once and for all. I thought that cutting his dick off would be the end of him, but I guess I was wrong."

The door suddenly blasted open and four of the bikers loudly invaded the quiet of Bernie's thoughts.

"Hey Bernie, what's happening? Why are you sitting in the dark and why's it so quiet in here?"

"Yeah, Bern. What's goin' on?"

Bernie just smiled and yelled out, "Nothing's goin' on guys. Here's some booze, have a drink," he held up a half filled bottle of Tequila, waving it back and forth. "Drink up, it's on me."

Chapter Sixty-Two

It didn't take as long to get back to Arthur as it did to get to Dream City. Lew walked into the kitchen where Linda had been putting up cans of preserves that he loved so much.

He walked up behind her, put his arms around her, and kissed the back of her exposed neck. She responded by taking his hands in hers and said, "Welcome back", and then she slapped his face, probably a little harder than she meant. However, she was furious. She had never asked before about his many disappearances, but this time she could not hold back.

"Lew, you know I love you to death, but where the devil have you been? I was out of my mind with worry, I even went to the police for help. So, where have you been?" she said this all in one breath and had to sit down from all her exertion.

"Linda, I know how much you have endured, and let me tell you all about it. At least what I remember."

She said at last, "Sit down, have a cup of tea, and tell me before I haul off and crown you."

"Ah, my trip, what an adventure. Yes, well I will tell you this, I found out a lot about myself and what is expected of me. You must believe that I have done nothing wrong, I'm talking about the recent goings on around town."

"Oh, Lew, I never thought otherwise."

"Well, I bet the police have a different outlook. They might think that I have something to do with the killing at the store and that I have done the cutting of that biker. But, I have to straighten them out on both counts. I guess I have to go over to the station and talk to them."

"Wait ten minutes, Lew. I think we have ten minutes to spare. After all you have been gone for days."

"I think we have ten minutes, and while these preserves are settling we can be doing something else," he said with a curious glint in his eyes and a suggestion in his voice.

"Hmm, yes. I believe we can," she smiled and turned to look deep into his eyes, "Yes, I believe we can," as she took off her apron. Their tranquility was ended abruptly as a car roared up to the outside of the house. Doors opened and slammed shut as the two detectives came quickly up to the front door and knocked sharply. "Lew Wallace, this is the police. We need to talk to you...now!!!"

"Oh, Lew. What is this?" Linda cried.

"Lew Wallace, come out now..."

"I'm coming, officer", Lew called out as he patted Linda on the back. "I guess we'll have to delay the quiet time for a while", he said as he went to the door and opened it to the detectives.

"Come on in, detectives", he said cordially.

"Mr. Wallace, we need to talk, but not here. Come with us, please," Ralph said.

"Okay, can I ask what this is about?"

"Not here, we'll talk at the station."

"Am I under arrest, Detective?"

"Not at this time. But we need you to come with us now, Mr. Wallace."

Lew turned to his wife and said, "Don't worry. I was going to go there anyway. Please call John and let him know where I'll be", he said as he kissed his wife lightly and left with Ralph and Alan.

Linda looked after him as he climbed into the back seat of the car and a tear formed in her eyes. "I hope they believe him," she sobbed.

Chapter Sixty-Three

The shadow had placed himself far enough away for safety, but close enough to make an accurate shot if the need arose. He was hidden behind a trash container across and adjacent to the bar where Bobby Pearl's gang hung out. As he waited patiently, he observed all kinds of leather and denim clad figures as they constantly came and went through the charred door that closed the bar to prying eyes. The only clue to what was going on inside was the half dozen to sometime dozen motorcycles of various sizes and makes parked in an orderly fashion out in front.

No noise or music pierced the peaceful façade of the bar, so no noise ordinance could be enforced.

The form was dressed mainly in black and stayed in the shadows of the container. He made no sudden moves to draw any unwanted attention to his being there.

His weapon of choice was a Heckler Koch 40 caliber rifle with a telescopic sight mounted atop its sturdy stock. He only needed one shot to get the job done. The other bullets were only insurance.

Being the expert that he was, he carried 20 extra bullets as a testament to his professionalism.

It was really dark when the shadow heard the roar of a Harley slowly rounding the corner and approaching the bar. He recognized Bobby's bike as soon as he saw it, and even in the pitch black, he believed Bobby Pearl was the rider.

Quickly he raised the deadly accurate rifle to his shoulder and took aim at the leather jacket of which he believed was his target.

Grinning, he squeezed the trigger and watched as the bullet ripped into the back of the jacket. He watched as the body jerked and fell forward, his left leg caught on the exhaust pipe on the side of the bike. The mass fell and brought the heavy motorcycle crashing down on top of the rider.

The shadow quickly faded back behind the container and made his way back to the car he had parked two blocks away. He slowly pulled out and drove away from the area. Smiled to himself at a job well executed and for the rest of the money Bernie was to give him. Or, so he thought at the time.

Back at the bar, no one heard the shot. Carl the Ripper happened to be leaving just as the body hit the pavement.

"Holy $#!+," he yelped, "Hey guys, get out here, I think Bobby's been shot," he called to the slowly closing door.

All at once, the eight members who had been drinking inside of the club stumbled out and stood over the now prone bloody form entangled in the bike.

"Is that Bobby?" one of the gang asked as Carl turned the body over.

"No!!!" Carl exclaimed, "It's Duanne. Somebody call 911! I think he's still alive!"

"But, that's Bobby's machine, what's Duanne doing with it?"

"Who knows? Maybe Bobby's not up to riding yet and he loaned it to Duanne. Makes sense."

"Did anyone call 911 yet?" Carl asked.

"Yeah, did it already."

"Wow, what a lousy break for Duanne. Poor dude."

"Somebody get me a towel or something. He's bleeding pretty badly", Carl called out to the gang.

Chapter Sixty-Four

"Alan", Ralph called out, "We've got another murder. A biker has just been shot outside the biker bar. No ID, yet. Let's go."

"Jeez, this is turning out to be more than just harassing young girls, isn't it?" Alan said shaking his head in disbelief.

"A lot more, partner."

"The locals should have the scene taped off by now," Alan said as they made their way out.

"I hope no one else was hit, but it wouldn't be the worst thing that could happen to that bunch," Ralph offered.

"No, I guess not, but we can't let anyone overhear these thoughts", Alan said in a low voice.

It did not take more than a few minutes to arrive at the scene. The detectives observed that all the motorcycles had been removed from the front of the bar, with the exception of Bobby's machine, which was encircled with yellow crime scene tape and was covered with Duane's blood.

No one was in evidence from the bike gang and the only ones standing around were the officers from the Arthur PD.

Ralph and Alan approached Sam Urban, and as they did, he detached himself from the other officers with which he had been conferring.

"Detectives, you got here really fast, I guess everyone in town has heard of this shooting already. Bad news travels real fast in a small town."

"Sam, who is it under the tarp?" the officers had spread a cover over the body mainly to preserve the evidence and secondly to keep prying eyes from viewing the body.

"At first we thought it was Bobby Pearl. That's his bike." Urban said, pointing to the overturned motorcycle lying beside the covered body, "But it appears Bobby loaned the thing to this poor kid who wasn't even a member of the gang…yet".

"Well, I guess it's just bad luck for him", Alan said a bit sarcastically.

"Yeah, I guess, anyway we think there was a sniper who hid down there by the trash container", he pointed to the container that was about 60 yards down the street.

"We found some candy wrappers and a shell casing. He must have been waiting for quite a while to make his hit."

"Some patience, sounds like a pro, another biker wouldn't have that kind of patience to hang around that long and be such a good shot."

Ralph said this as he knelt at the body and inspected the entry wound, "It looks like a large bore rifle, the hole is a through and through," as he turned the body slightly to check the exit hole.

"That's what we thought," Sam Urban said.

Chapter Sixty-Five

"Gee Nurse Mary, it was nice of you to put me up in your apartment, and I really do need to take the time to heal. You won't be sorry you took me in," Bobby Pearl said in his sexiest voices ever.

"Oh, Bobby, don't you worry your cute little head about it, I have plans for ways to get paid back", Mary said with a hint of a smile playing at the corners of her pursed lips.

"Oh, and I can't wait," Bobby purred, not knowing yet that without his precious package he could only talk about it, he still believed he was capable of performing as usual.

Nurse Mary Tyler knew, but she had her own plans for Bobby and they did not include sex, but they did include his penchant for committing certain non-legal acts for her and placing the blame entirely on him. She definitely had plans for Bobby Pearl.

"Uh, Mary, do you think you could change the dressing on my er, crotch?"

"Yes, just lie back and let little Mary take good care of you, just relax, baby," she said sweetly.

Bobby laid back and in the back of his mind he thought, "Oh man, did I fall into a good thing here. This chick is really in love with me. Man, what a deal, I'm going to run this out as long as I can, oh man, wow!!!"

She looked at him lying back on the sofa with that smug smile on his face, like a cat that swallowed the canary.

She smiled to herself and thought that he was going to pay for the girls he raped and harassed for all those years, "Yes, he will pay."

"Mary," he called out "Get me a beer."

"Okay baby," she said obediently, took a cold one out of the refrigerator, and brought it to him with a smile on her face.

"Thank you honey," he said "I love how you take care of me."

He turned on the T.V. and sat up almost straight as the news came on and the scene at the bar showed a covered form next to a bike that looked suspiciously like his own.

"And reports of a shooting have resulted in the body that you see covered up here on the street" a news reporter pointed to the sheet covered body.

"It is reported to be in retaliation in the biker community for what is reputed to be a feud. Further details at 5:00 o'clock, when the Police Chief will issue a statement, now back to the station with other news of the day."

"Summubich," Bobby yelled out.

"What's the matter Bobby?" Mary came rushing back to the living room, a concerned look on her face, "Did you hurt yourself baby?"

"No, no", he said, quite agitated" Just the news on T.V. don't worry about it".

"I do worry about you, it's not good to get upset, is there anything else I can get you?"

"Yeah, another beer," he said, a nasty little sneer on his face.

"Okay love, you got it," she said.

"Man, am I glad I'm here and nobody knows where I am", he said to himself.

Chapter Sixty-Six

Bernie Tampon looked at his choice of assassin and railed at him, "Dammit, you got the wrong guy, Bobby's still alive".

"I did what you instructed me to do. I shot the guy that rode up on that Harley. How could I know that Bobby let that jamoke ride it. At that distance he looked exactly like Bobby."

"Yeah but, and this is a big but…it was the wrong guy…now what are you going to do about it."

"Nothing, I did the job you sent me out to do, if your info was good, it would be over, and as you say, but, I don't do make-ups. It's still your problem not mine, and may I say, you… still owe me."

"Oh right, you want to get paid for failure, I don't think so… pal." Bernie said with a little bravado, something he rarely showed.

The shadow man advanced on Bernie, and stuck his face up close to him and snarled, "Bernie, don't forget what I do for a living, and I'm saying to you, you better get me my money…NOW!!! Or, I will do a job here for just the principle of it… DO- YOU- GET- IT"… he added with a sharp jab to Bernie's chest.

Bernie thought for the briefest second that maybe he pushed this guy a little too far, and with what seemed an eternity he said, "You know you're right, I did screw up," and as he swallowed the large lump that had formed in his throat he added, "Don't get so upset, I'll get you your money."

"That's better, because you know I know where you live, go get it …now."

"Right, wait here, I have to go to my bank, I'll be right back."

"Okay, but no funny stuff, got it Bernie," he said with the emphasis on Bernie's name.

As he left, Bernie's mind was in turmoil, he had to think of some way not to pay this banana and live to enjoy his life. He knew he had a pistol in the safe deposit box, but would he have the guts to use it. He had never shot the thing, ever.

He jumped on his bike and as he did he also thought of just taking off for parts far away and unknown to anyone, but as soon as the thought entered his head it was washed away with the knowledge that this guy could and would track him down and wouldn't hesitate to kill him and not pleasantly at that.

He rode to the bank, sweat dripping from every pore, and as he entered the bank, he was manhandled by two Arthur policemen.

"Wha, what is this, what the hell are you doing," he bellowed.

"Sir, you are hereby requested to accompany us to police headquarters, if you refuse and if you resist we will be required to place you under arrest. So, how would you like to do this sir, easy or otherwise, it's up to you, sir."

"But you don't understand, someone is waiting for me and I can't keep him waiting", Bernie said in a whiney voice, much afraid of what the shadow man would do if he did not show.

"That's not our problem sir, you need to come with us", said the larger of the two officers.

Bernie's mind was whirling, he thought that this would definitely screw him up, but then again, maybe the safest place for him to be right now would be in custody. He could wrap his mind around either option. He decided finally to go peacefully with the two cops.

"Okay, guys, I'm yours," he said and quietly left the bank with them.

Chapter Sixty-Seven

While this was happening, Lew and his wife were sitting quietly across from each other. Lew was trying to explain to her exactly what happened to him when he enters the fog. He was not doing the greatest job of it, mainly because he himself did not fully know precisely what it was.

"I only know, that time doesn't seem to matter. The flow of things appears to be a natural progression. I pass by places and sometimes I stop and talk to people and experience certain situations, and then I move on without rhyme or reason."

"This last time, and I agree, it took a long time, and to tell you the truth, it was bizarre. I was in a place called Dream City, and I think I contacted ...myself... I know, it sounds crazy, but this persona thing told me it was my conscience and it was there to tell me some things that perhaps I had forgotten, things about myself. Linda, am I crazy, am I, I know it sounds crazy, a person travels far away and talks to himself, and sees places that do not exist, has got to question his sanity, and don't you think?"

"Lew, the only thing I can say is, I don't think you have anything to question, I don't think you're crazy or mentally unbalanced, I just think you are a special person. You have not done anything to harm another human being, you have helped so many people it's hard to count how many. Lew, don't beat yourself up about this thing, this fog thing, as long as I understand and I love you it doesn't' matter."

"I don't deserve you Lynn, and I promise you that somehow I will find out why I have this condition and maybe somehow learn to control it, even if I have to get therapy of some sort to fix it."

"Lew, we will work it out together, I am 100 % behind you."

Chapter Sixty-Eight

"Police Department, can I help you", the duty officer answered the 911 call.

A gruff voice greeted him on the phone, "Yeah, I know who iced that biker last night."

"Excuse me, sir," the officer said, "May I have your name and number, just for our records, sir?"

"You gotta be kiddin, Mac, nah, I don't think that's a good idea. Do you want the info, or not?" the caller snarled.

"Yes, of course, sir. But, can't you give me your name, please?"

"Do you want the shooter or not?" another snarl from the caller.

"Okay, sir. What is the name?"

"Fred Heinz, they call him Ketchup. Get it? He's a killer for hire."

'Fred Heinz, okay. Do you know where we can find this person?"

"You might get him at the Cross' bike club. I hear he hangs out there. But, he's going to be carrying, if you know what I mean. You do, don't you?"

"Oh, yes, sir. I certainly know what that means, but don't you want to..." at that, the caller hung up the phone and the officer sat there with the receiver dead in his hand.

He immediately buzzed the detective's office and reported what had just happened.

"Do you have the recording of the call, officer?" Ralph asked.

"Yes, sir. Its protocol to record all 911 calls. I'll have it sent up to you ASAP."

"Good man," Ralph said.

"Alan, get ready, we have a call with the name of the shooter." Ralph called out. "I hope its Bernie Tampon," Alan opined.

"We'll see, the tape is coming up right now."

Almost immediately, an officer brought a tape to Ralph's desk.

Ralph inserted it into the recorder and both Ralph and Alan listened with rapt attention.

"Who do you think the caller could be? It's obvious he's disguising his voice, I don't recognize him." Alan said.

"Wait listen, he's just trying to sound tough, like he's an old biker. But, it sounds a little like the Poet. Listen to some of the inflections, he rolls his R's a little. You can't disguise your voice 100 %, something always comes through. My bet it's him."

"I think you're right Ralph, now that I think of it, it does sound like him."

"Fred Heinz, Fred Heinz, where have I heard that name before?"

"Ketchup, man, these guys, if nothing else they are inventive with their nicknames, but it all seems apropos." Alan said, scratching his head with frustration.

"Okay, Al, let's get whoever is available and get over to the Cross' place. Maybe we can nab this character."

Ralph called the Chief and requested all available officers to join him and Alan.

"Let's go Al, we got the OK from the chief, the troops will be downstairs in five. We'll fill them in and head over there."

"Okay, Ralph, I only hope this isn't a wild goose chase."

"We've got to check it out anyway, wild or not. Let's go."

They checked the load in their weapons and left to join the troops downstairs.

Chapter Sixty-Nine

The raid on the Cross' barn turned out to be a bust. when they arrived the place was as empty as a fully eaten Dunkin Donuts 12 pack. The place had been cleaned out. Ralph and Alan cursed the 911 caller up and down.

Not to be discouraged, Ralph suggested they take a ride to Bernie Tampons clubhouse and was given a thumbs-up from Alan and their troop.

All the members of Bernie's biker club were sitting around playing cards, watching TV, or just talking between themselves. Bernie Tampon was nowhere in sight, as he was in custody at the station. No one had seen him since yesterday when he jumped on his machine and roared off without a word to anyone. None of the bikers knew that he was being held, and that was the way Bernie wanted it.

Ralph, Alan, and the six officers in their troop fanned out in front of the bar. They had pulled up without sirens or strobe lights.

Ralph had instructed the existing bikes be chained together to impede the hoods from taking off.

When that had been done, Ralph took out a pre-filled warrant that allowed him to enter the bar legally and hold anyone he needed for questioning.

He motioned to three of the officers to cover the rear as they approached the front door.

"Police, everybody up against the bar," Ralph announced as he pushed back the front door, "All hands out in front and on the bar, NOW!!!"

"Hey, what's going on, you can't do this", a denim covered pigtailed, heavily whiskered mammoth of a man yelled out."

"This is a police raid and we have a legal warrant, so shut up, and do as you are told or you're under arrest for resisting a legal order. Do you understand?" Ralph countered.

"Where is Bernie Campon?" Alan asked as he frisked the bikers for weapons.

Various sizes and shapes of knives and truncheons were taken in the pat down and thrown onto the bar.

No one said a word as they were faced with heavily armed police.

"I asked 'where is Bernie Tampon?' Answer up or you're in contempt of a legal warrant." Alan repeated.

He looked over the group of eight grubby men, "Okay, let's take them all in, and let them stew behind bars for a couple of days".

"Okay, okay," piped up the mammoth biker "Don't get your balls in an uproar. We haven't seen him since last night. We don't know where he is."

Ralph smiled to himself knowing exactly where Bernie was, but not letting these jokers in on it. He wanted all the information he could get.

Smiling inward he said, "Somebody knows, you tell me who might know and we will go easy on you creeps."

The large man looked around and then shook his massive head, making strange little objects fly from the mass of hair, "There's no one here that knows any more than what I told you."

"Okay, cuff them all," Ralph called out, "Until someone talks they are all under arrest, Alan, toss the back room and see if there's anything we can use, and don't be neat about it."

Alan briskly walked out of the main bar with two officers and pushed in the back room door roughly.

"Wait, you can't do this. We didn't do anything wrong, we were just sitting here doing nothing," one of the bikers yelled out.

"You are all carrying illegal weapons and are impeding a police investigation, that's how we can do this, unless somebody talks." Ralph said over their raised voices.

"But we don't know where he is" several said.

"Get them out of her. The bus should be outside by this time."

Ralph joined Alan as they were all led outside to be loaded onto the police bus.

Chapter Seventy

The eight bikers were herded into interrogation rooms at the station, and a seedier group had not been seen there in a long, long time, if ever.

While they were being processed, Patrolman Sam Urban approached Ralph and Alan as they were filing out the necessary paperwork for their roundup.

"Detectives", Sam started as he neared Ralph, "I think I found a clue".

"Really, Sam. And, what makes you think that?"

"Well, as we were combing the area behind the dumpster I looked all the way under and came up with this," he said as he held up a plastic baggie with a shell casing inside.

"Wow!!!" Ralph said, his eyes opening a little wider than usual, "Alan, come over and see what Sam here found out there".

"Yeah, I thought it might help, maybe there's a print on it. Maybe we can match it. What do you think?" he said looking back and forth between Ralph and Alan with a gleam in his eyes and appearing to be rocking to and fro in front of the two detectives.

"Maybe, if there's a print on it and the print is in AFIS, (the fingerprint analysis system). Let's get this to the city. ASAP."

"I'll run it up myself. If that's alright with you?" Urban said expectantly.

"Er, umm, what do you think Alan? Can we trust this guy with an important piece of evidence like this?" Ralph asked Alan, as he shook the little bag in his face.

"I don't know, Ralph. Maybe we should have them come down here."

"Well, okay guys, whatever you decide", Sam said, looking sadly at them.

"Sam, don't worry. You can take it to the forensic lab in the city, as long as you don't lose it on the way. Do you think you can do it?" Ralph asked him with a slight smile on his usually poker face.

A huge smile broke out on Sam's face and he practically danced in place, "You really mean it? You guys really trust me? I'll get going right now, man. Thanks, guys. Trust me, I'll get it done, and I hope they can find something on it."

Sam almost raced out of the squad room, Ralph and Alan looked at each other, then Alan said, "Remember when we were that young and eager?"

"No," Ralph said chuckling.

"Well, let's get back to work. There's enough laughs to go around with these bozos."

"Right, I'll take the bozo in interrogation #2, you can have your pick of the litter," Ralph said as he gathered his files.

"Guess who gets the first deal going?" Ralph said as he entered the room with a bearded biker sitting forlornly in the metal chair behind the metal table.

Chapter Seventy-One

Bernie Tampon was in a panic, the shadow man had completely disappeared, and Bernie didn't know where he could possibly strike next, since he had not been fully paid for his screwed up assassination of Bobby Pearl.

Even though he supposedly had the protection of the Arthur P.D. and was in this protective custody he didn't feel secure. He felt the shadow man could reach out and find him. His gang offered him no guarantees that he could be safe, as they didn't have a clue where he was. But, even if they knew, they would probably abandon him if they knew he was behind in the attempt on Bobby's life.

He thought he would need them more than ever, the Cross was looking to knock them off, the cops were looking to disband them and charge them with the killing at the store. Bobby is nowhere to be found, but he did not think he would be any help with anything since he was so injured, especially by Bernie's own hand, if and when he found out.

"Okay, Bernie, just to be up front with you, we have a witness and evidence that you killed the Cross member at the store and that you are the one that tried to kill Bobby Pearl--not once, but twice that we know of. So what do you have to say to us?" Ralph said as he sat in front of the biker.

"I got nuthin to say to you detective, as a matter of fact, I want my lawyer," Bernie said as he looked smugly at Ralph.

"Okay, Bernie But, let me remind you of what I think you already know that once you invoke your request for an attorney you won't be able to tell us we are wrong and you won't get whatever deals we make with the other guys for their part in this mess. We also have no reason to reveal who has been the witness against you, that is until your trial and believe me the District Attorney will nail your leather clad ass to the wall."

"Jeez, you play hardball, don't you detective?"

"Yes, I guess I do, especially when it's murder involved. I kind of think anyone who would do that I play the hardest ball you have ever seen."

"I still think I want my lawyer," Bernie said and then closed his eyes and his mouth.

"Okay, you got it", Ralph said as he closed the folder he had walked in with and left the room.

"Alan, what have you got?" he called out.

"To tell you the truth partner I don't have much. I have one guy that looks stupid, but I get the impression he knows something. He doesn't look like much, but then none of them do. Let's you and I back him up to the wall and press him hard."

"You got it, pal. I'm ready when you are."

As they proceeded to the interrogation room, the Chief waved them over to his office.

"Guys, I've been bombarded by calls from the citizens. They are up in arms. It seems that bikers have been coming in from outside of the city limits. They have been creating havoc on the little store owners, they get drunk, it's like the Wild West out there, and I don't have the people to handle it."

"Okay, Chief. I'm going to call New York and have them send in some reinforcements. We'll cut this thing short in no time, and I, we apologize for the problem," Ralph said.

"You think the city will send help?"

"Oh, you know it. We have all the support we need."

"Okay, Ralph. I'll tell everybody it will be taken care of, and thanks."

"No problem, Chief. Now if you'll excuse us, we've got some pressure to apply on someone."

"Go right ahead, gentlemen, and good luck."

As Ralph and Alan turned to leave, Ralph said to his partner, "We sure stirred up some kind of a hornet's nest out here, haven't we?"

"That's for sure."

"Okay, let's stir some more. Bernie wants his lawyer, so he's on ice for now. But, he's only one player that's bad for sure. I know we can pin most of the garbage on him. So after we talk to your guy, we'll deal with him some more."

"Do you think he'll call an attorney, or is he just bluffing?" Alan asked as he gathered his file and a tape recorder.

"Remains to be seen, pal. We just have to wait", Ralph answered as he turned the door handle to the room.

"Okay, show is on", Alan said as they entered the room.

Chapter Seventy-Two

"I think we have to get Lew Wallace in here again, Al. I'd like to know just where he has been these last few days. Maybe he has something to do with the recent shooting. I really don't think so, but still, I'd like to know." Ralph finally said as his eyes started to droop from fatigue.

"It doesn't sound like something Lew would do, you know. He's more about thinking before doing something as sneaky as bushwhacking someone with a rifle. Do you know what I mean?" Alan said looking directly at Ralph as he said this.

"I know, Al. But, he's been absent and the shooter has all but disappeared. It's very odd, both gone at the same time, coincidences happen sometimes. But, this is very close and I'd like some answers. Do you agree?"

"I guess we could use one or two," Alan responded.

"Okay, let's go over to his house and see".

As the partners got up to leave, they were paged from the desk downstairs. Ralph picked up the phone and after a few seconds, he signaled Alan to take a seat.

"What's up?" Alan asked as he sat down heavily.

"Lew's downstairs and Davis is bringing him up."

"Wow, talk about coincidences. Right, partner?"

"Maybe too much of one, I don't know."

Officer Pat Davis escorted Lew Wallace off the elevator and led him over to the detective's desk and he left almost immediately.

"Good afternoon, detectives," Lew said softly.

"Good afternoon, Lew", Ralph said, holding off on asking why he was here.

"I think there's something you need to know, my wife suggested I come in and talk to you. I don't know if you are aware that I have been gone for a few days, a week to be exact."

"A week you say?" Ralph asked.

"Yes, well I know it was a week because it took me a while to get where I eventually ended up. Let me explain", Ralph and Alan sat quietly while Lew chronicled his trip To Dream City for them. When he stopped talking he looked from Ralph's face to Alan's, but he could not gauge what effect his story had on them.

"I'm sorry, have I said anything to you that makes you think I'm not telling you the truth?"

"No, no, Lew, we are just wondering", Ralph started to say when Alan touched his arm and motioned with his head for Ralph to follow him out of earshot of Lew.

"Ralph, does this story seem a little bizarre to you?"

Ralph countered with, "I don't know, but it could be so weird that it might be true. How could anyone make up something like that, unless..." he left his statement hanging.

"Okay, let's see if he's got anything else, and then we'll ask him some questions."

"Okay, let's go," Alan said.

They came back to Lew. He sat stiffly in the metal chair and looked expectantly at the two detectives.

"Okay, Lew," Ralph started, "Let's go over this one more time. You say that you somehow enter a sort of fog, and when you do, time has no sense of passing, that you kind of lose reality for an undetermined length of time. This time you appear to have left your home, and you don't know how you got there, and at one point you found yourself somewhere in New Jersey. You spoke to a person there, you can't remember who. But, then you went to a remote location called Dream City, where someone told you to look into yourself to find your way in life. Then all of a sudden the fog appeared again and you just found yourself back home. Do I have that right?"

"Pretty much, Detective, but anytime this fog overcomes me I find that I do somewhat beneficial things that afterwards I can't remember them."

"And you don't remember helping a young girl that was being beaten by four boys or stopping bikers from raping two girls in the park."

"No, I don't, sir," Lew said.

"We have people who have identified you as the Good Samaritan that did these things."

"I'm sorry, detectives. I understand what you are saying, but I only remember the fog and nothing I do after that."

"You do realize that this is a very strange story, and you can understand our reticence in believing it. Can't you?" Alan spoke up.

"Yes, I do. And, to tell you the truth, I find it difficult to understand and believe it myself, but this has been happening since I was a very young child. At first I was very frightened by it all, but when people kept coming up to me and congratulating me, I began to think that, maybe, it wasn't a bad thing."

"Mr. Wallace, Lew, I'm sorry to put you through all of this, but we have two murders to solve and you disappearing has us asking these questions," Ralph explained.

"I understand, Detective. And, I know you have a job to do, I'll cooperate in any way I can," Lew said.

"Good, thank you, Lew. You can go now, but keep in touch, okay?"

Chapter Seventy-Three

Shelly Fallon, the secretary to Assistant District Attorney Ralph Jackson, answered the persistent ringing of the red telephone in his office, "ADA Jackson's office, may I help you?"

"Yes, Ms. Fallon, this is Detective Bloom calling from Arthur. I think we need some legal assistance up here. It seems that some of our perps have invoked their rights to talk to an attorney".

"Have any attorney's shown up yet?"

"I have it on good authority that one or two from the city are on their way pretty soon."

"Okay, I'll notify Mr. Jackson."

"And, we might need some backup in the way of manpower. There are factions of other biker gangs from out of town on their way here, also."

"Alright, Detective. I'll have a couple of teams sent up there forthwith. Is there anything else you need while we are talking?"

"Hmmm, you might want to have a psychiatrist on tap. There are some really , and I'm not qualified to assess them, but maybe you could call them... crazies."

Shelly laughed at that and replied, "Well, Detective, I think you've seen your quota of unstable characters in your time, so maybe that qualifies you to some extent, don't you?"

Holding back a laugh, Ralph said, "As a matter of fact I guess you're right, and please Shelly, call me Ralph, detective sounds so stiff."

"Okay, Ralph, I'm sure we don't want something stiff between us."

"Hmmm, you're quite correct there, Ms. Fallon," Ralph said in a joking manner, hoping she understood his humor.

"Okay, Ralph, I understand. And, now, back to business, I'll get right on your problem and I'll get Mr. Jackson informed of what's happening up there. And, Ralph, why don't we get together when you get back to the city, if that's okay with you?"

"I see no reason not to, Shelly. I'm looking forward to it."

"Then it's a date, so to speak, right?"

"You can count on it."

She hung up and looked around at the austere office that she occupied, "Whew," she blew out the breath she had been holding in for the last few moments, "I am getting to be quite the femme fatale, suggesting those things to him. I wonder what kind of man he is, oh well, soon enough."

She called her contact at Police Plaza One for the extra manpower he requested.

After that, she walked over to the door separating ADA Jackson's office from hers, she knocked lightly and then walked in.

"Shelly, what can a harried ADA do this morning for you?"

"The detectives we sent to Arthur need some legal help with some of the accused that have requested their attorney's."

"Okay, let's send some junior assistants there and if they need something higher I'll take the trip, but let's wait and see what transpires."

"Sounds like a plan to me, sir. I'll get two juniors rounded up. It will be good experience for them."

"Good, get it done, and then come back in, I need your expertise on a case."

She nodded and briskly walked out the door while he stretched his back in his executive chair.

Chapter Seventy-Four

Three black SUVs pulled up in front of the station, five uniformed New York Police Officers stepped out of the first car and fanned out in the street. Three civilian clad detectives and one smartly dressed female departed the middle SUV and started the short walk into the station, the female in the lead.

Two officers with three K9 dogs sat for a few minutes in the third car, waiting for word to go into the rear of the station where they would feed the dogs and wait for further orders.

The three detectives and the woman approached the front desk and introduced themselves, and asked for the Chief and Ralph Bloom.

The officer of the day asked them to wait while he called upstairs to the detectives and the chief and directed them to the benches.

Two minutes later Ralph and Alan came down and greeted the detectives, Alan glanced at the gaggle of lawmen and then focused on the lone female, something about the back of the woman seemed familiar to him, and as she turned to him, he recognized her. It was Gina Grant, the FBI agent that Ralph had hit it off with on one of their cases. She had been transferred to another state after the conclusion of that case and they had a rather protracted long distance relationship since then.

"Ralph", Alan interrupted his introductions to the new arrivals "Check out the female over in the corner, the one with her back to us".

"I see her, Al."

Ralph turned fully in her direction and without warning he shouted with more gusto than he ever displayed usually, "Gina, Gina, what are you doing here?"

He rushed over to her and took her roughly in his arms.

"Excuse me, sir," she said with a slightly shocked look on her face, belying her joy at seeing him.

"Oh, I, er, pardon me. I thought you were someone I once loved?" Ralph spouted.

"Oh, Ralph, you're so easy to kid", she said, her voice muffled by his face that was nuzzling her's.

"I'm so glad they sent you."

"Who else would they send when federal laws have been broken, and especially when the other attractions are already present?"

Ralph looked at her with curiosity, "Federal laws? I wasn't aware of any federal laws that had been broken around here."

"Oh, yes," Gina said "Interstate homicide and kidnapping are the laws that have been attributed to your friend Bobby Perlow, the Pearl, as he is commonly known."

"I haven't been aware of any kidnapping, and the homicides we are still sorting out."

"After we secure Bobby Perlow in custody and we establish that all our facts are straight, we'll be taking him back with us to D.C.," she said in an officious tone.

"But before we take him back you and I need to talk."

"Sure, but didn't we already do that a while back before you reported back to D.C.? I haven't heard from you since then. I thought you forgot about me. To tell you the truth I've had you on my mind a lot lately."

Gina looked at him and sighed, "Ralph, sweetie, I haven't forgotten our last night and I'll never forget you. How could I?"

"But, then how come I haven't heard from you? Every time I call, I get the FBI runaround at Langley. They toss me back and forth on the phone for so long I get a little frustrated I just hang up. I guess that's just what they want out there, you know."

"Yes, my dear. I know and I'm sorry."

"Okay, now that you're here and that's been cleared up. Can we get back to the case?"

"You're right, and the FBI takes precedence, so let's get to it before anything else," Ralph said as he handed her his files.

Chapter Seventy-Five

"Oh, Bobby, you're such a hoot," Nurse Mary shrieked.

"Yeah, I used to be more of a hoot, but since my operation I can only be a little peep, if you know what I mean," Bobby lamented.

"Oh," gushed Mary, "Don't you fret yourself about that. You know that's not the only thing that is important in a relationship."

"Is that what we have, a relationship?" Bobby asked as he looked deep into her sky blue eyes.

"I was hoping that it was," she said, looking back at his handsome face.

"Wow, I mean, jeez, Mare, I mean I never had what you call a real relationship before, you know what I mean, I always ran from those things, I've been on the move so much and I went from place to place. Don't get me wrong, I think you're great and I want to be someone you look up to, but if we are to be, you know, together, I have done things that probably you might not want to hear about," he said as softly as he possibly could.

"Bobby, I know some of the things and I know there are more things that you feel you should tell me, but, you don't have to if you don't want to right now."

"I know that's how you feel right now, but when you know all the things I've done you might not feel that way."

"Oh, let's not borrow trouble. Let's just enjoy what we have now."

Bobby took her in his arms and kissed her lightly on her eager lips, "Mary, I really like you and strangely enough I only want to make you happy, I only wish I could do more, you know what I mean?"

"I know Bobby, I know," she said as she got up and prepared to go, "Now I don't want to leave you, but I have to go I have a job you know."

"And," Bobby said, "I don't want you to leave either but I also have to go, I have to go to the police station and talk to somebody. They may want to hold me for a while, will you wait for me?"

"Do you really have to go right now, can't you wait a little while longer, and you silly goof, how can you ask me that question after the conversation we just had?"

"I guess I can wait a little longer baby." Bobby said with his old swagger.

"I love when you talk tough, that way you're such a bad boy Bobby Pearl," she said coyly, winking seductively.

"Oh no, don't do that, it drives me sort of crazy, if you know what I mean, so come over here and I'll do the only thing I am able to do for you." he said as he licked her lips.

"Oh Bobby, you're so bad!!! ~" she murmured, removing her robe to show what she had been thinking about all along.

Sounds of satisfaction could be heard throughout the house, but the sounds could not compare with the pleasure she felt. This pleasure was not hers alone.

Chapter Seventy-Six

Bobby Pearl stared bug-eyed as Mary shed her robe. He could not believe his eyes and his monumental luck. Her breasts were full, and to his mind, perfect. The areolas around her swollen nipples were like ripe cherries and he could not resist, he took the right nipple in his mouth and suckled for a long luscious time, what he thought, and an eternity. He could not get enough of her.

Mary stroked his rich brown hair, recently washed and smelling like the apple scented shampoo she had bought for him. She smiled in satisfaction as he practically sucked her nipple off her breast.

His hand traveled down between her legs and she moaned loudly as his fingers found her already wet private place.

He looked up at her face, which was contorted with pleasure. She was not a particularly beautiful woman, but he liked what he saw. Her eyes were a pale blue, so pale it seemed like you could look right through them, her hair was a dark brown, almost like black and the combination was unsettling, but not unattractive. All in all, he considered himself very lucky to have her in his life, especially at this point and in his condition.

"Bobby," she whispered.

"Yeah, baby", he responded.

"Can I do anything to help you, you know, with this?"

"Mare, you know the only thing I can do is pleasure you, I don't think I want anything else right now."

"But, Bobby, I feel so selfish."

He sat up abruptly and looked deep in her eyes, he touched her lips with his and said, "All of my adult life I have been taking advantage of women, first girls and lately helpless women, and only now I feel so bad that I did those things. You took me in and did it because, I don't know, either you took pity on me or you're just a good person. Whichever, I kind of think you saved me from more than this," he pointed at his groin area. "You saved me, I think, from being worse than I was to be better than I was. I don't need anything more right now than just being with you and giving you pleasure. Do you know what I mean?"

Looking at his handsome face, holding it between her two hands, she said, "Bobby, I understand, you do not need to say any more. I think we found each other just in time, don't you?"

"Yeah, baby, I really do. But, let me say one more thing. You know when you first took me in I had some bad thoughts, thoughts about how I could use you and take advantage of you kindness. I know, I was really looking out for Bobby, and only Bobby. But, being with you and knowing how good you are, those thoughts are completely gone and I'm, I guess, different now."

"I know I really miss my, thing, you know. Really because I don't want to deprive you of what you truly deserve. I mean, you've given me so much and I really feel bad that there's nothing I can give to you."

"Oh, Bobby, I don't expect you not to feel badly. I understand about your problem, but it's no problem for me. You can satisfy me in that special way and I know how much you miss what you should have and maybe sometime in the future it can be replaced. But, you have to bide your time right now. And, I have a confession to make. When I first took you in it was not because I felt sorry for you. I did it for another reason, and a reason that now I have changed my mind about. I originally wanted to have you here under my thumb to make you pay for all those things they say you have done. Things that you also have told me about and now I don't want to do that anymore. I find you are more than that, and you are a better person.

Unexpected tears fell from Bobby's eyes. He was not accustomed to this type of emotion and he turned his face away to avoid her seeing them. He choked back the lump that had formed deep in his throat, but his shoulders heaved as he tried to hide his sobbing.

"Bobby, don't," she said.

"Can you leave me alone for a while please, baby?" he managed to say stuttering slightly.

"Of course, but you don't have to feel bad. I think I love you!!!"

"Thanks, I'm working things out about you and I appreciate you're saying that."

"Okay, so now I have to go to work. I'll leave you alone until later."

"Thanks, baby. Have a good day."

As she left, she planted a fat juicy kiss directly on his lips.

He looked sheepishly at her as she left. It would be his last look at her, but he didn't know it then.

Chapter Seventy-Seven

Lew entered another fog, he was drawn to the back door of the abandoned barn that housed the Cross' biker club. All appeared to be quiet except for a slight rustling inside. He circled the barn until he found a small door in the very back. It had been used in the past as a pass through for the delivery of small items, such as towels, cases of beer, and some deliveries of weapons.

He nudged the door with the toe of his shoe and it swung partially open, enough for him to see a foot or two inside.

Poking his head around the doorframe he heard two people talking, they were not being particularly quiet, as they evidently did not expect anyone to overhear them.

"You better pay me now Enis, or else the same thing that happened to Bernie might happen to you."

"Oh, no it won't, pal. I know more about you than you think. I can have you put away permanently and no one will ever be there to bail you out, get it?" Enis had menace in his voice.

"Bernie was stupid, he didn't cover his ass and I can tie you to the Bobby thing. You forget, I got the scalpel that you used and it doesn't take much to let it fall into the cops hands. So, don't you be stupid, too. And, pay what you owe me, and we can both go away with no one the wiser."

The voices sounded familiar, especially the one asking for the payment. Lew knew he had heard it many times, but for some reason right at that moment he just could not place it.

He knew that one of them was the notorious Enis, the one they called the Penis, but echoes in the empty barn gave him pause to recognize the second man.

"Okay, Chief," Enis said finally, "I'll get you your money by tomorrow night, just hold off on everything, and get those detectives and especially that FBI chick off my back. "

"I'll do my best. You know I have very little control over the FBI, but I can sidetrack them for a while if I have to. You get me my money and then we'll see. Otherwise you're in for a whole lot of grief, do you get me Enis?"

The voice finally came to him, Chief Davis, the Arthur Chief of Police. Lew knew he had to get out of there as soon as it was possible without tipping them off that he was there. He took a step back, not noticing the empty beer can, it crunched loudly in the near empty barn, and skittered across the floor into the center of the bar room.

"Who the hell is there?" boomed Chief Davis's voice, "Come out now. I have a gun. This is the police, come out now or else."

Lew turned and ran quickly around the side of the barn and ran for his life.

Enis and the Chief came storming out the front door. It was by sheer luck that Lew had taken a route opposite the front and bolted over a low fence past the rear of the barn.

He kept to the shadows and managed to put distance between himself and the Cross' barn.

He momentarily stopped to catch his breath, he was not used to such exertion, and he felt a stitch in his side. He bent at the waist and sucked in much needed air.

Sounds of heavy footfalls could be heard in the front and side of the building where Lew was resting. He straightened and recognized the aura of fog that had controlled most of his life. He stepped inside the edge of the fog and understood that as long as he was inside no one could see him. Once inside he relaxed and watched as the Chief and Enis ran from side to side, trying to find whoever had been spying on them.

"Where the hell did he go?" Enis yelled.

"He's got to be around somewhere, there's no place to hide around here. Everything is boarded up or closed tight since the detectives got here. Let's have a look over here," he said, pointing to a furrow that crossed the field about 20 feet away.

"We gotta find him, he musta heard what we said and he probably knows who the hell we are. Don't you get it, we got big trouble now!!!"

Chapter Seventy-Eight

Three NYPD officers led by FBI agent Gina Grant approached Nurse Mary's apartment. Gina was flanked by the cops, as she knocked sharply on the door.

"FBI, we have a warrant, open the door."

She rapped again and repeated, "FBI, open the door. We have a warrant, Bobby Pearl. Open the door or we will be forced to break it down, open up…now…"

A slight sound, as if someone was stumbling around greeted their ears.

"Bobby Perlak, if you are in there open the door," she repeated.

"I'm coming, I'm coming, hold your water", came from behind the door.

"I got to put my pants on, gimme a sec, will you?"

"Get ready guys," she said as she stepped back slightly and to the side of the door, "This guy has a history of extreme violence, so be ready".

"Yes, ma'am. We understand," Officer Harvey Dean said as they all released the snaps on their holsters.

Locks were undone and the door opened slowly, every man on the outside stiffened with tension in readiness for action.

Bobby Pearl stood in the open doorway, shirtless and shoeless, his eyes widened in surprise at the totality of the police force before him.

"What's up? He asked with an innocence that belied his guilt."

"Bobby Perlak, we have a warrant for your arrest, step outside, and place your hands behind your back, please," Gina ordered.

"What charge are you arresting me for?"

"You'll hear the charges at the station. Right now place your hands behind you," Gina repeated.

"Okay, but I want my lawyer. I'm coming with you, but you can't ask me questions until I get my lawyer."

Officer Harvey Dean placed handcuffs on Bobby and led him out to the squad car, placing him carefully in the back seat.

Gina sat in the passenger seat while Dean took the driver's seat and quickly drove off.

Bobby sat quietly in the back, hung his head, and mumbled to himself as they passed his former stomping grounds.

"Bobby, just so you're not so in the dark. I'm going to go out on a limb by telling you some of the charges against you are federal. That's why I'm involved. You know that the locals have their own charges, but I take precedence over them."

Still silent, Bobby lifted his head and stared at the back of Gina's head, wishing she would just shut the hell up. He worried what Mary would think when she came home and found him gone, all his personal possessions still there, and virtually untouched.

The short trip ended at the police station where he was roughly hustled out and pulled through the front door to face practically the entire Arthur Police Department.

"Welcome, Bob," Chief Davis said sarcastically, "Come right in, we saved a room for you. Please come in and make yourself comfortable," he said as he clapped him on the back and ushered him into an empty cell, removing the cuffs, and tossing them back to Officer Dean. He slid the cell door closed on a startled Bobby Pearl.

Chapter Seventy-Nine

"Well, now that we have both gangs in lockup I think we have Arthur's problems solved," Alan said.

"Right, Alan," Ralph said sarcastically "But, we still don't have the shooter from the outside of the bar, if no one owns up to the identity we're still far from finished.

"We and the Chief have a lot of interrogations to perform. Most of these characters have no clue, but we have to weed them out one at a time," Ralph told his partner, although it did not need to be said.

"Then I think we should start interrogating."

"I'll take Bernie and work on him, you can have the pick of the crabgrass guys," Ralph said. "And the Arthur cops can do the Cross gang, but I think we have a shot here with this bunch."

"I also think Gina should be privy to all the different groups, she has a definite edge on the Arthur cops so that's a big plus for us."

"Okay, let me go and give everyone their assignments and I'll be assisting the questioning by the local cops," Alan said as he set off to address the Arthur P.D. about what they need to accomplish.

"Bernie Campon", Ralph called out to the de-facto leader of the gang, "Come with me".

Bernie pulled himself up from the iron bench that he was occupying and ambled after the detective, his face contorted in pain.

"Room number one Bernie, step lively, I don't have all day and I'm not in a particularly good mood", Ralph ordered.

He sat Bernie in a hard metal chair facing a huge mirror. The mirror was, of course, a two-way and everybody who watched Law and Order or any cop show knew that the mirror was always two-way and could be observed through it.

"Man," Bernie started off by saying, his face flinching with nerves. "I know what's going on, and I got nuthin' to say".

"Take it easy, Bernie. I just want to ask a few easy questions. And, if I hear what I want, you most likely will be free before you know it. If you jerk me around I will get a little mean, do you get me?"

"Oh, okay, what do you want to know? I ain't got a lot of time, I need to be on the road you know."

"Yes, Bernie, I know. You are anxious to be away from this town, and you're very nervous. I can see that, but what I want to know Bernie is why you are so nervous. What has crawled out of the woodwork and gotten under your skin?"

"Nuthin's under my skin, I just like to be on the road."

"This I can understand, Bernie. I also understand that there are factions that want your skin, and they will not stop until they get it. Isn't that right, Bern?"

"I don't know what you're talkin about."

"Oh, come on, Bernie. I've heard the talk. I know you're scared out of your wits and you only want to split this town for faraway parts."

"Oh, yeah, what have you heard?"

"Well, that's something I wanted to ask you about. You know I have the authority to lock up your whole bunch and probably the entire Cross gang, but I would like to see you get a deal here."

"Oh, yeah, what kind of deal?" Bernie sat up in his chair with a look of expectation etched across his screwed up face.

"Well", Ralph hesitated, "For the right information I could find it in my heart to go very easy on you".

"What kind of information?"

"Okay, Bernie, let's stop jerking each other around. You know what I want, I want the shooter and I want the guy that killed the creep in the store, give me either one and we have an understanding. So what is it going to be Bernie?"

"I'm telling you, I got nuthin'. I don't know either of those things, and maybe you should ask Enis the Penis, that's his kinda gig."

"Okay, Bernie, if that's the way you want to play it, there's nothing I can do for you", and with that Ralph got up and left Bernie sitting forlornly in the cold damp room.

Chapter Eighty

George Freemont was an attorney from Manhattan. He was not one of the prominent types of lawyers that one would associate with a big city lawyer. In contrast to a respected barrister, George was more the ambulance chaser type who represents the lower class of clients, such as Bernie Campon.

"Bernie, you didn't say anything that they can use against you, did you?"

"Nah, George. I don't think so, but they grilled me pretty good. I can't remember half the things they asked me and half the things I said."

"Listen to me, Bernie. From this point on, you don't say anything except your name and nothing else. Tell them, and I'm sure you already have, to speak to me, no questions. Got it?"

"Yeah, I got it. But can you get me outta here? I don't like being cooped up in no jail."

"I'm doing the best I can, Bernie. Just hang tight."

"Yeah, hang tight--it's easy for you to say."

George Freeman looked exactly like one would expect for a person who represents known low-lifes and felons. He wore a well-worn sharkskin suit that sagged at the knees and the elbows. His once sparkling white shirt was sort of a dingy off-white now and it seemed he had spent some of his hard-earned fees on a brilliant orange and blue polka dotted tie. The suit, of course, was shark grey with two-inch out of date lapels and cuffs that hung down below the heels of his black clumpy shoes.

In other words, he fit the typical look of a sleazy ambulance chaser to a tee working out of a storefront office on Canal Street in downtown Manhattan.

The office was as neat and tidy as George was, and had exactly one secretary and one telephone line.

George Freemont Attorney Ltd. was well known in the world of the criminal element.

Notwithstanding, George had in the past represented some of the most heinous mob related hit men and, because of his failure to get them off, he was to be relegated to this lowly position in his legal life.

Now, Bernie Campon (aka) Bernie Tampon was looking for him to get him out of the mess in which he was so deeply mired.

There was little hope of George being successful, but old habits die-hard.

"Bernie, you realize that what you're faced with, I mean, the charges are pretty substantial and it's going to take a lot of money to even post a fair defense. I know, I know, you're innocent. But let's be realistic, I know, and you do to, that the evidence is compelling against you."

"Yeah, but George, I also know that you almost always have an ace up that sleeve of yours, so don't bull$#!+ me about money. You can always hit another client for extra cash."

"That's what you think. Those clients are long gone. I'm living hand to mouth right now, so you have to see about financing this thing on your own, otherwise I can't do too much of anything for you. You know I'd be right beside you otherwise."

"Dammu, George. I've been in this crummy jail and unless you get me out there's no way I can make any contacts. You just gotta get me sprung."

"Okay, I hear you. Maybe I can make some kind of deal with the judge, but we've got to find out who is behind these cops getting all this overwhelming evidence against you. Be patient."

"Sure, it's easy for you to say, be patient. You're out there and I'm in here and you ask me to be patient, ha." Bernie said this so fiercely that George backed away to the cell door with his briefcase clamped to his chest in real fear for his life.

"Be patient!!! I have no more patience," Bernie roared so loud that the officer on duty rushed to the cell door with his hand on the butt of his weapon.

"Bernie, Bernie, take it easy man," George said meekly, still holding his briefcase in front of himself for protection.

"Hey", the officer yelled as he approached the cell, "Hold it down in there, you", he said to Bernie. "Back off and get back to the wall, you," he pointed to George, "Come out of there, right now."

"You got it officer. I don't want to be here another second. Open the door, please," George pleaded, sweat breaking out all over his body and trickling down his spine.

"George, don't leave me, I need you man," Bernie pleaded as he sat back on the commode at the rear of the cell.

"I'll be in touch, Bernie", his voice receding out of the cellblock.

"Yeah, sure." Bernie said sadly.

Chapter Eighty-One

Ralph sat pensively at one of the empty desks at the rear of the detectives' room. He had not yet grasped that after all of the interviews he Alan, Gina, and the Arthur cops had conducted, they seemed to be almost back at the beginning instead of further along in the investigation. There appeared to be a leak at some point that stopped everything cold.

He sat picking at a cuticle on his left hand, his mind had gone over the situation several times, and the case was still at a standstill.

"Alan, could you please come over? I need to run something past you", he called to his partner, his mind still racing with facts but no answers.

"What's up, partner?"

"Alan, I'm up a tree here. Everywhere we turn we run into a roadblock. There's something or someone that's standing in the way. We need to go over everything with a fine-toothed comb, but I'm getting an itch that someone close to us is the problem."

"Okay, I got it. Let's start from the beginning. We were assigned to assist the Chief and do whatever was necessary to clean up the town. So far, we've had a break-in and a murder, girls being molested by biker gangs and another outright sniper related murder, plus a sexual assault resulting in a pervert's penis being forcibly removed, something I don't think he gave up willingly. How's that for a recap?"

"You're forgetting the fact that we have a Good Samaritan or vigilante. However, you want to label him. Who says he goes into a fugue or fog state and doesn't remember what he does when he's there."

"Right, but that's really not an issue at the moment. Whoever is blocking us has to be a principal and has to be in a position of authority."

"From the Mayor on down, no one is innocent, we have to treat everyone equally, and look deeper into backgrounds. I've got an idea in the back of my mind, but so far nothing is in concrete." Ralph said in a thoughtful way, his brow furrowed as in confusion.

"Do you really think the Mayor might be involved?" Alan asked.

"Alan, I'm suspicious of everyone, except you and me."

"Well, partner, I'll get our tech's to run some backgrounds on each and every player here. If there is anything to find they will find it."

"Okay, Al. And in the meantime, I'm going to re-interview more of the townspeople. Maybe I'll turn up something."

With that, the two detectives separated and went to ply their tasks.

Chapter Eighty-Two

George Freemont had been successful in getting Bernie released with the caveat that he could not leave town. As a further precaution, an officer was stationed by the biker bar just to insure he did not leave.

Nowhere that Bernie turned after he was released was safe, his eyes practically rolling in his head. He had developed a pronounced facial tic that made it seem as if he was winking when anyone looked at him. His hands trembled and holding a hot cup of coffee became an exercise in futility.

In so many ways, one could say, that without too much of an effort Bernie Tampon was literally falling apart.

Besides his trembling hands, facial tic, and an all-consuming headache and stomach gas, Bernie's mind had been on speed dial, thinking that around every corner there was someone or something that was out to get him.

He had every reason to think that way since his principle protector in the town's police department, the Chief, had left him with the cryptic words, "Bernie you either have to leave town or your death is extremely imminent."

Those words had sent him over the edge of sanity and he reacted in a way that no one had ever seen him react.

This disturbed all but one of his gang, almost to a man. The guys started to gather their worldly goods and silently they packed their motorcycle saddlebags and made ready to move at a moment's notice.

Bernie, in his stupor and severe mental state, noticed nothing but possibly a little activity that he passed off as natural from his guys.

The one member not affected and making no moves was a small and understated man who had joined the gang almost one year ago. In that year, he had made no close associations with any member of the gang. He kept to himself and if he was noticed at all, it was not evident to Bernie or even Bobby when he was the leader.

Alex Soose (aka) Doctor Seuss, sniffed slightly and sidled up to Bernie, so as not to startle him. It did not work, Bernie jumped as if he had a hot poker stuck in his ass.

"What, what?" Bernie yelped and backed away.

"Easy, Bernie. It's just me, the Doc. I just wanted to see how you're doing, I noticed you're a little stressed and I thought I could help."

"Help, how can you help me?" Bernie whined and shrank further away, his face contorting in multiple tics.

"Easy, easy, Bernie, you got to chill."

"Chill, how the hell can I chill, I'm so f*@%@d, Doc. I can't tell whose coming for me or where their coming from. How the hell can I chill?"

"I know, pal. But, you got to calm down and think. It doesn't help if you're wound up so tight you can't think. You know what I mean?"

"Doc, I appreciate that. But, it's coming from all sides and it's driving me crazy. I just want it to go back to the way it was last week. You know what I mean?"

"Sure, sure I do. But, I'm here for you, Bernie. Just remember that."

Bernie slumped down on the legless sofa that they had stolen a year ago and put his head in his hands, tears flowing from his reddened eyes.

"Doc, could you please leave me alone for a while? I need to think."

"Okay, Bern. You sit there and think," he said as he moved around behind the sofa.

From his back pocket, he quietly pulled a length of piano wire with two ends wrapped in foam and secured with electrician's tape.

He unfurled the wire and swiftly encircled Bernie's neck, pulling the wire taut and practically severing his head from the rest of his body. It took mere seconds and Bernie Tampon was no more.

Doc uncoiled the wire, wiped it clean of blood on Bernie's sleeve, rolled it up, and secured it back in his pocket.

He walked quickly, but not too quickly out the back door, mounted his Harley, and rode out of town, leaving as quietly as he had come.

Chapter Eighty-Three

Bernie sat with his back straight on the sofa. There was no indication that there was anything amiss when two of the biker gang walked in.

Dave, one of his oldest friends, and Carl both stopped in front of him. The light was dim in the bar and, without thinking, Dave said in his most intrusive voice, "Hey, Bernie, what's happenin' how the hell are you doin' now that they sprung ya'?"

Not getting a response, evidently because Bernie no longer owned a voice, Carl chirped in, "Yeah, Bern, you must be relieved".

Still nothing from the body.

"Bernie, hey, is everything okay?" Dave shouted.

He walked closer and shook Bernie's shoulder, thinking, "Boy he must really be tired and sleeping".

As he shook the shoulder again, Bernie's head flopped forward and a black liquid spilled down the front of his shirt, and then there was this foul odor.

"Damn", Dave yelped and jumped back.

Carl, who was behind him, also jumped only because Dave had yelped so loud it startled him.

"Carl, its Bernie. I think he's dead. Look, I think that's blood." he said pointing to the pool at his feet.

"Jeez," Carl said awestruck, "What the hell happened here? We were outside only a few minutes. What the hell happened?"

I don't know. But, I do know we better get the hell out of here, and I mean pronto, brother."

"I'm with you on that. Let's split, man."

As they rushed out the door Dave said, "I wonder who did that to old Bernie?"

Carl said, "I don't have a clue, and I don't want to meet that dude. I just want to get the hell out of here...fast."

Chapter Eighty-Four

Ralph and Gina were having a rare luncheon date at the Ambrosia Restaurant on the main street of Arthur. They were re-living an old case they had worked together regarding computer theft and murder that had reached a bloody but satisfying conclusion.

They were also reminiscing about the short, but torrid, affair they had enjoyed prior to

Gina being transferred to a higher position in Washington, DC.

Regrets for their short-term affair poured out from both of them, but nothing was being said at the moment about re-establishing their relationship. On the other hand, the looks they gave each other belied their feelings for each other.

Just when Ralph was about to broach the subject of that relationship his cell phone insistently buzzed.

"Alan, you're interrupting a quiet, well deserved moment, so it better be good."

He listened, his smile turned down and a frown formed on his brow. Gina knew the message was not a good one and she immediately began gathering her belongings, ready to move out.

"It's not good, another homicide," Ralph said sadly. "Maybe we'll get a clue this time, it's Bernie Campon".

"I'll get CSU over there ASAP, where is it?" Gina asked pulling her cell phone out.

"The bar they used as their headquarters," he responded, snagging his car keys from the table.

Since they were only two blocks away, they arrived before CSU had a chance to get there.

"Alan", Ralph called out through the open door of the bar. "Come on out, CSU is due any second."

No answer came from inside, gingerly Ralph peeked inside, there was no one there except for the form on the sofa.

"Alan", he called out, louder this time, "Where are you?"

"I'm out back. Come around the side, I'll meet you there."

Ralph and Gina went around the side of the building, dodging empty liquor bottles and discarded bent and crushed beer cans, plus a messy trail of different sizes of broken glass.

"Watch your step," Ralph cautioned Gina, "You can get a nasty cut around here."

She merely nodded, thinking to herself that he seemed to have a need to protect her, even though her FBI training had prepared her for more than broken glass.

Alan was bent over what appeared to be a deep rut in the ground just outside the rear door.

"It looks like the perp left in one big hurry. He burned rubber leaving."

Ralph and Gina squatted down next to Alan and checked out the surrounding area.

"He left a good boot impression over here," Gina said pointing to a perfect shoe impression in the wet ground.

"Okay, another biker. But who's giving the orders to clean house?" Ralph mused.

"Somebody wants everyone involved to be uninvolved, in the worst way."

"Looks like it. I think it would be a good idea to get Bobby Pearl and put a protective guard around him. More than one man, if it's not too late." Gina said, "I'll call the Chief and have him send two of his officers to stay with him".

Chapter Eighty-Five

"Urban", Chief Lewis called out, "I need you to find Bobby Pearl, lock him down, and sit on him until I say it's safe."

"Okay, sir. But, do we know where he is? The last I heard he was still in re-hab."

"Well, he's not there anymore according to the grapevine, so you've got to track him down. When you do find out where he is call me. Say nothing to anybody, only me. Got it?"

"Yes, sir. I got it."

Officer Sam Urban went out the side door of the station and commandeered a squad car. He powered up the on board computer and scanned the internet for the GPS unit they had installed in Bobby's jacket collar.

The red dot flickered on and showed a constant stationary signal indicating that Bobby was not moving.

Officer Urban started the car and proceeded the one mile to where the signal indicated the GPS unit resided.

Little did he know that the unit had been discovered by Bobby. He discarded it in a dumpster far away from where he was at the time. In hindsight, he had saved his life for the time being.

When Urban arrived at the spot where the GPS unit lay deep inside the dumpster, he looked around… confused.

"What the," he murmured to himself as he looked around and saw…nothing…but an empty lot with just a lone dumpster sitting in the middle.

He walked over to the dumpster, a little uneasy, not knowing what he would find. He half expected to see a body in the trash and thought that it wouldn't be a surprise, especially the way bodies had been piling up around town lately.

Swinging the cover open, the odor of trash assailed his nose…only trash…no rotting body was discovered on top. He used his baton to push aside mounds of garbage and spied the brown leather jacket with the gang's logo on the back. He fished it out gingerly with the baton and laid it on the ground.

"Chief Lewis", Urban called on his car radio, "I'm sorry to tell you this, but Bobby's in the wind. I found his jacket with the GPS in a dumpster on Forsyth Street, no buildings around, just an empty lot."

"Okay, Sam. Come on back and we'll think of where he could be holed up, over."

"Yes, sir. Over and out."

Little did the Chief or Officer Urban know, Bobby was the guest of the FBI at that moment.

Chief Lewis sat back in his big leather executive chair and clasped his hands behind his huge head. He mulled over the events that lead to the debacle that he himself had created in his desire to become the next mayor of Arthur.

His decision to drive the biker community out of the town, make a bigger name for himself, engender the town's loyalty, and possibly the majority of votes would make his dreams come true.

"It has now," he thought "become the worst decision I have ever made. There is no turning back now, especially with two NYPD detectives and now the FBI everywhere I turn."

The problem for him now was to cover his tracks and creep out from under the noses of everyone.

He could not have everyone killed off, with the exception of the last two. The one who was contracted to do away with Bobby and, if he was successful, then he would only have one more to deal with.

Chapter Eighty-Six

"I'm beginning to suspect that there's more to this than what we were sent here to do," Ralph said to Gina and Alan.

"I am, too. There's just too many killings for this to be the minor crime spree that One Police Plaza made it out to be," Alan added while he was shuffling several files around, trying to arrange them in chronological order.

"But what could be gained? Most of the bikers have picked up and left. One too many have been targeted and put out of the picture, and I really can't blame them. But, who's behind it all? Bobby Pearl? No picture of innocence there. The only one who had any real power is the only one left. And, since he'd been replaced by the now dead Bernie, who else is there to be concerned about? Certainly none of the wacko's who have been paraded in here to smell up the place."

"I agree," Ralph said, "So who is left? The guy that offed Bernie and shot the clown in front of the bar has probably gone long ago. So who is left that could profit from all this crap?"

"The logistics of this thing is being managed by someone who has been in on this from the beginning. But, for the life of me, I can't seem to get a hold of him in my head." Ralph said.

"Maybe, just maybe, he's someone that has been in plain sight all this time. You know someone that we see every day and never give him a second thought," Gina added as she sat looking at the murder board with all the players and their names tacked to it.

"There are so many characters involved. Some have been jailed, a few killed, and a lot more have taken off for parts unknown. So who does that leave?"

Ralph joined her at the board, and as he stood beside her, he could feel the warmth of her close proximity to him. He felt the same desire for her even though he had not seen her for a year or so.

"Gina, do you see anything that might strike you as more than unusual up here?" he said, only to break the feelings that were in his mind about her and got back to the business at hand.

"I know you have a keen mind and see things that we sometimes overlook."

"Hmm," she thought to herself, "I know there's something on his mind besides this case. Funny, it's been on mine, too."

"Well." There was a pregnant pause before she spoke again, "I was wondering if possibly someone, in law enforcement could be involved."

"Gina, how could you even think of such a thing?" Ralph said sarcastically, "Someone in the law enforcement. Wow, where did you come up with that?"

"I don't know. But, you look at this board and you delete all the knows and all of the incidentals, where do you go? There is an unknown element that been orchestrating everything, and to my mind the only other thing that's possible is…law enforcement."

"Okay, let's work on that premise. Who do we know here that could possibly have the influence and the wherewithal to pull this thing off…?"

"Only one," Alan chimed in as he joined the two of them and pointed to the top of the board.

"No! That can't be…What would his motives be?"

"It can't be, but it's the only other alternative. Who else can be the one?"

"Okay, you guys. Let's be smart about this. WE don't share this with anyone until we have positive proof, right."

Alan and Gina nodded their approval as they all moved away and sat at their desks, shuffling files. All with their own disturbed thoughts.

Chapter Eighty-Seven

Lew was chewing his inner cheek, deep in thought. He was trying to figure out how in the world that knife had wound up in his pocket. He did remember going to the park, but only as a vague memory. The events that happened during the fog were lost to him, but the aftermath was clear. What he did recall was one of the bikers that ran with Bobby Pearl had come unreasonably close to him after Bobby was dismembered. It did not make a lot of sense then, but now…it sort of dawned on him that it was the opportune time for someone to plant the knife on him.

"But why?" he thought to himself. "Why would anybody do that to him? I have only tried to help people." Then, he recalled that not everyone appreciated what he had tried to do all his life.

"Linda", he called out, "Linda, could you please come in here. I need to run something by you."

As she walked into the den where he sat behind his makeshift desk, she noticed he was leafing through a cluster of papers.

"Is there anything I can help you with, dear?" she said, wondering what he had on his mind, which lately was confused.

"Yes, these papers are from people who know us. All of them are saying they want me to run for office here in Arthur. Do you think they're serious?"

"Well, I think all of them believe you have done good things for this town, and they would like to see you rewarded for those things. And, yes, they are serious. Why do you ask?

"I don't know, but what I do know is that someone had targeted me to be discredited. You know, the knife incident and other things that cast suspicion on me for things I haven't done."

"Lew, don't lose sight of who you are. You're incredibly respected here by most of the people and I do suspect that you may have enemies high up, I mean politically."

"You know, I think you're right. Someone doesn't want me to be regarded for a political career. Although to tell you the truth, I never mentioned anything like that to anyone because I never had that type of ambition… until now."

"Are you thinking of it now?" she said with a slight smile on her face, knowing what a laid-back person he was.

"It certainly has given me pause for thought, I tell you that," he said also smiling, possibly for the first time in a long while.

Linda looked at him smiling and said, "Lew, I think you would be an asset to this town in any capacity. Is there an office you are thinking of?"

"Not at this moment, but I will be thinking real hard from now on".

She walked over to him as he sat and placed her lips lightly on his and said, "Lew, I love you. And, I'm very, very proud of you." She then left him alone to think. She smiled her way back to the kitchen, humming to herself.

Lew watched her leave and turned back to the letters he was holding in his very capable hands, the seed fomenting in his head.

Chapter Eighty-Eight

Doc Seuss, who in reality was working for Chief Lewis (undercover as a biker), was the only person that could put the Chief in a dangerous position since the chief was behind every illegal act in the town.

In reality, Doc Seuss was Officer Tony Garcia, who could fit in with any group of bikers in the country as his hobby was motorcycling in faraway locations other than Arthur. He was known by a variety of aliases in such diverse groups as the Devils of San Francisco, the Angels of Casper, Wyoming, and many other groups and places, and never once was pegged as a cop.

Tony was a not a hale and hearty guy at 5' 7" and weighing only 160 lbs. But he worked out on a regular basis.

He had a wife once, but was divorced and then somehow widowed at the age of 26. The demise of his wife aroused no suspicion since he had taken all precautions to make it seem as to be an accident.

Brakes failed at the most dangerous time when she was rounding a precarious turn on the side of a high mountain in upstate New York. The road happened to be slick with ice, and there was nothing she could have done to prevent the car from careening down the rocky escarpment to her death.

Tony Garcia had shared his home on the outskirts of Arthur with a waitress who never asked questions about his off-duty occupations and was always available to his desires. She was three years his junior, and even though she worked long hours on her feet, she would accompany him to dances and other police functions.

Sharon Baker, his waitress, was a buxom blond with a penchant for smoking thin cigarillos. It made her look like a throwback to a whore from the old Wild West, and if she decided to don a bustier, it would not have surprised Tony one iota. In fact, he sort of preferred her that way.

Sharon worked at the local diner from 11:00 in the morning until around 8:00 at night. The schedule afforded her the luxury of sleeping late in the morning. Never once in their relationship did she ever ask about his comings and goings. She relished the times when he worked long hours and sometimes when he left for days at a time, since she neither loved him nor desired his insistence for sex. She wanted it when she wanted it and got it when he was there for it.

This was one time when Tony was away on some case, as he called it. And, she appreciated the time to herself.

Tony, in the meantime, had been about 50 miles away in a cabin high in the mountains, a cabin that he and the Chief had maintained as a sort of a safe house. This time it was a safe house for him. The place was stocked with food, enough booze, plenty of firewood for the fireplace, and an old potbellied stove.

There was plenty for him to occupy himself with a large flat screen TV with all of the extras he could ask for and an assortment of DVDs ranging from hardcore porn to games that required no intelligence whatsoever.

He was not concerned about being discovered because the cabin was so remote. The nearest neighbor was more than five miles away.

He slept when he wanted and ate when the need arose. His only concern was the loneliness and the lack of sex.

He also kept in touch with the Chief via cell phone and was encouraged to stay put until further notice, which he intended to do for as long as it took.

He had no idea that the Chief had other plans for him and was preparing to implement them sooner rather than later.

Chapter Eighty-Nine

Ralph, Alan, and Gina sat before the murder board. None of them spoke. They just stared at all the facts and bits of evidence in front of them.

Ralph pulled at his lower lip in consternation. He was perplexed when Gina said, "Clearly, there is something we are missing here".

Her analytic mind, that had served her well at the FBI, was almost blank at this stage.

"We know the problem is high up the ladder. Whom do we know here in Arthur that wields enough power to set all this in motion? Who has the knowhow to be the orchestrator of such a complicated mixture of unconnected crimes?" Alan interjected.

"This is getting more and more complicated every time we look at it. Maybe we should call in a fresh eye to gain a different perspective. I think I have a man in mind, someone who's not in law enforcement." Ralph offered. His voice took on a different tone as he said this.

Alan looked at Gina, and then they both looked at Ralph.

"Who do you have in mind?" they both asked at the same time.

The only man who has been here and has claimed to see everything and who has been a sort of local hero for a lot of years...Lew Wallace..." Ralph said in all seriousness.

"Lew Wallace. Man, I never thought of him. Wasn't he a suspect at one time?" Gina asked.

"Well, yes, for a brief moment. But, we ruled him out almost immediately. All you have to do is talk to him for about an hour or so and you'll see." Ralph said earnestly.

Gina mused, "Lew Wallace...yes, I can see why you thought of him. But, how do you think he can help?"

"It seems that sometimes he goes into what he calls a deep "fog". He sees things. He can travel to places and suddenly everything is clear. He can see, hear, and act as he sees fit."

"Do you think he will be willing to come in and help?"

"I can only call him and ask. It's up to him entirely." Ralph retorted.

"Okay…let's give it a shot," Alan said as they gathered around the phone.

"Hold it! Let's not use the station's phones. Let's go somewhere and use my cell phone. I'm not so sure the phones here are secure," Ralph said quickly as they walked out together and left the station house.

Chapter Ninety

Chief Lewis watched as the trio left the station. They had their heads together for a long time and he expected and hoped they would include him in on their conversation. Unfortunately, they had not. He sat back, lost in thought.

"What did they have that made them leave in such a hurry?" he worried.

As he thought, he began to set in motion his plan to open up talks with his backers with respect to the upcoming mayoral campaign. They were several city officials who had shown an interest in the chief, as his record, with the exception of the last few weeks, was quite respectable.

"I hope these detectives and that FBI *b!+@#* won't *f*@%* up my plans," he said between clenched teeth as he buckled his service weapon on his waist and perched his chief's hat gingerly on his head.

The Chief had put in his time, first as a patrolman in Chicago. He rose to lieutenant and then captain by the sheer force of his ability to ferret out the main players and major criminals from the street scum whose activities were insignificant in the grand scheme of things.

He retired with honors and was hired by the town of Arthur, which was a relief to him. In Chicago, his name had been on the lips of some very bad mob figures that had more or less painted a target on his broad back. He had heard the rumors and decided that putting in for his retirement was in his best interests.

The attraction to Arthur was the low percentage of crime, which was about 10% annually. The hiring of peace officers was left entirely to his discretion and he brought two former colleagues from the Chicago P.D. with him. They proved to be ultra-loyal to him.

Lewis followed his longtime beliefs that criminals were to be treated sternly and taken out of circulation permanently, or otherwise, as the case may be. In this case, it would be most prudent for him to get rid of any person or piece of evidence that could implicate him, no matter how trivial it might turn out to be. That meant Doc Seuss had to go, not away elsewhere, just away…permanently.

He picked up his cell phone and stood behind his desk, facing the wall where dozens of plaques graced, praising his past victories and performances, pictures showing him with various politicians and personages of note.

He spoke briefly, and then turned back from the wall with a hint of a smile on his weathered face.

Chapter Ninety-One

"Lew, I know we've been on your case before. However, we have come to the conclusion that you are clear of any wrongdoings. We've come to you to ask for your help. I know, that is, we know how you have this ability to enter into a fog state, and you can do this by invoking it yourself. What I mean is, can you? Can you call this on yourself, or do you have no control of it at all?"

"Well, detectives, I'll tell you this much, in the past, I have probably caused it to happen. But, I don't know how I did it."

"Usually I have no control. It comes upon me and I just go with the flow, so to speak. Why do you ask?" Lew responded, more than curious about Ralph's motives.

"We ask because it appears that someone, aside from the biker gangs, have to be in a position of authority and is controlling all the crimes around here. We're not sure about how high up the chain it goes, but it only seems logical to us that not mere bikers are behind this."

"And, what, may I ask, do you think I can do to help you?"

Ralph suppressed a chuckle and said, "We're not sure what or how you can help. We were hoping that with your ability to go places without anyone being aware you are there, might be an alternative. What do you think, Lew?"

"Oh, and you think I have the ability to choose where and when I can do this. Is that correct, Detective?"

"That's something I can't answer. But we were hoping you could. By the way, my name is Ralph, and this is Alan and Gina. Please, let's be on a first name basis."

This time Lew suppressed his own chuckle. "Okay, guys. I think it would make things a little easier. Well, now, let's see if I can help. I don't know if concentration works, but let me go someplace quiet and work on it. Whom exactly am I supposed to be concentrating on? Anyone in particular?"

Ralph looked at Gina and Alan with a puzzled look on his face.

"Lew, to tell you the honest truth, we haven't zeroed in on anyone in particular. We're on a sort of fishing trip here, but I would personally look into someone with a law enforcement background, since our every move seems to be anticipated. It could be someone in the town's hierarchy. You know someone who gets our reports as soon as we send them in. I'm also thinking of not submitting daily updates in hopes of keeping our stuff to ourselves. That way we know what we know and no one else will. I'm also thinking that whatever we report not be 100% true, possibly to make this person tip his hand somehow."

"Okay, guys, let me go and see if I can conjure up what you need." Lew said as he moved to leave.

The trio looked at his back as he left and in unison they said, "Good luck, Lew."

Chapter Ninety-Two

As Lew entered the front door of his modest home, his wife Linda ran up to him, hugged him tightly and said, "I'm so glad you're back home. I couldn't help but wonder what the police wanted you for. They didn't harm you in any way, did they?"

"Oh, no, my love. They only wanted my help."

"Your help, how can you help? Are you sure?"

"Well, I believe that they think that when I go into my fog state I can go anywhere, and by doing that I can find the person who is behind the crime spree here."

"But, Lew, can you do something like that?"

"I don't know. I've never tried to channel it. It has always seemed to come when it comes. There might be a way, but I'll be darned if I know how."

"Well, whatever happens, Lew, I know you'll do the right thing. You always do," she said as she noticed a faraway look in his eyes.

"Lew, are you feeling alright? You look sort of strange."

"I don't know, Lynn. I'm feeling kind of tired. Maybe I need some sleep. I'll just go up and see if I can take a little nap. Will you be okay?"

"Yes, you go and don't worry about me. I'll be right here."

"Okay," he said as he lumbered slowly up the stairs to the bedroom.

She watched him go with more than a little concern. He had never acted this way before, and she worried about him.

Almost immediately, he fell into a deep sleep.

Chapter Ninety-Three

Chief Lewis was lurking around the corner of his office, listening to Ralph talking to Lew and the others.

His first impression was that it was a foolish attempt, but when he thought about it further, he became somewhat concerned.

"What if…," he thought… "What if there was something that Lew could do to control his actions?"

He paced back and forth, thinking. He rifled through several files, trying to come up with an available plan to alleviate the crisis in his brain. He knew he had to contact his undercover operator, Doc Seuss, and try to stifle the situation.

Slowly he concluded that Seuss had to go. He had to make sure that there was no one that could connect him to the killings, and to make it look like he was the one that solved everything. To hell with the NYPD and that FBI *b!+@#* that was tagging along with them.

Finalizing his thoughts, he slipped out the back door. Taking his personal vehicle out of the lot out back, he slowly drove out of town.

Chapter Ninety-Four

"Okay," Ralph said, "I don't think we can wait for Lew to come up with his fog thing, but we can progress in a slightly different way. Let's focus on prominent people who would profit from everything that's gone on here, especially since we got here. The only one I can think of is the Chief. But, before we accuse anyone, we've got to build a tight case, otherwise we'd be making laughing stocks of ourselves. What do you guys think?"

"Well", Gina piped up, "I certainly don't know if the Chief qualifies. He's only been the most helpful and has put himself out a lot to help us. You know, with the manpower and whatever forensic help he could offer. He even assigned that nice patrolman, what's his name? Sims, Simon, no I remember Simmons. He tried to guide me through the weirdo's that were involved in the store robbery. That reminds me, I haven't seen him around for a while. I wonder where he is. You know, he was always kind of underfoot all the time and he knew just about everything we were planning to do. Hmmm, I wonder."

"You could be onto something, Gina," Alan said. "He was always the go-to-guy when the Chief needed information doled out. Do you think he's been on patrol lately?"

"I don't know, but maybe the Chief does. Let's ask him," Ralph said, but in the back of his mind he had something niggling there about the Chief and Simmons. He couldn't nail it down just then though.

The trio marched single-file to the Chief's office. Alan lightly rapped on his door, once, no response, twice, same result.

Ralph tried the door and found it open. When they looked inside, they found an empty office.

They looked at each other, and in turn, nodded their heads knowingly.

"The Chief is always here at this time," Ralph said as he turned around and strolled out of the office.

"I wonder where he's gotten off to? He said as he walked to the front reception desk where Officer Urban happened to have desk duty this morning.

"Sam, have you seen the Chief this morning?" Alan asked.

"Yes, sir, he is in his office, I saw him just ten minutes ago in there."

"You didn't see him go out?"

"No, sir. He's supposed to be in there. Did you look, sir?"

"Yes."

"Oh, right," Sam said "Maybe he went to see the mayor or one of the chief's advisors. You know he's about to make a run for mayor this next election. He does a lot of work on his campaign."

"His campaign, does he spend a lot of time on that?' Ralph asked.

"Well, yes, he does. Every afternoon he's holed up in his office on the phone with whoever, I, of course don't listen in. But, he's on it a lot…why?"

"Oh, nothing. We were just going to brainstorm some ideas with him, and he's not there."

"He sure didn't come out this way," Sam said.

"Okay, no problem. We'll just get back to him later. Thanks, Sam," Ralph said as he motioned Alan and Gina to follow him outside.

He and the others walked three blocks in silence. When they reached the corner of Third Street, Ralph whirled around and faced them.

"Doesn't it occur to you that there's a lot going on that's a little strange?"

"What are you getting at, Ralph?" Gina said.

"What I'm getting at is that there may be an underlying theme here. Whoever can undermine the political powerbase could, in effect, take over and run things. They could make way for any changes they want and to make and bring in any element they want into this town. There could be big profits for someone who has the ear of the financial bigwigs."

"But, who would this someone be, pray-tell?" Alan asked knowing full well who Ralph was talking about.

Ralph looked at the two of them with a twinkle in his eyes. In unison they all said, "The Chief of Police and Mayoral hopeful."

"Right…"

Chapter Ninety-Five

Chief Lewis knocked on the door of the cabin where his man, Tony aka Simmons aka Doc Seuss had taken as a safe house.

There was no answer. He knocked repeatedly with no result. Going around back, he did not see Simmons' car or his motorcycle. But, he knew that as a longtime police officer and undercover cop, Doc would never leave evidence that he was where he was staying, especially now that he had been told to stay out of sight.

Lewis found both the front and rear doors were securely locked. He wondered to where his man had gotten.

"Damn," he said aloud, "Where the hell is he? I told him to stay out of sight, but this is ridiculous."

He searched the little copse of woods at the rear of the cabin but found nothing to show that anyone had been out there for at least two years.

Little did he know that Simmons (Tony) was lying prone on a hillock about a half mile away, watching through binoculars. He watched Lewis as he stomped around kicking up dirt as he tried both doors with no success.

He laughed to himself, thinking that he had done the prudent thing in leaving the cabin when he did. He had his suspicions that the Chief was all about cleaning up his business and that meant that he was the newest target to be cleansed.

Simmons was relieved to have escaped Lewis's plan and had prepared by packing all his gear and bringing it with him to his hiding place. His motorcycle was covered with branches and leaves and hidden behind him.

All of a sudden, his cell phone rang. At first, it startled him, as the only one who knew this number was the Chief. He scanned the screen and sure enough, it was the Chief, and with a great deal of trepidation, he punched the answer button.

"Chief, what's up?"

"Where the hell are you? I was out to the cabin and you weren't there. Where the hell are you?"

"I'm out of here."

"Yeah, I understand that, but I want to know where the hell you are. And more than that, where are you heading?"

"Okay, Chief, I'll tell you what. You tell me why you are looking for me and just what you're planning, especially for me."

"Simmons, I'm only looking for you to update you on what's going on and how things are panning out. So, I'm asking again, where the hell are you?"

"Do you think I'm that stupid, Chief? If you do, you're not as smart as you think you are. I know that you have to get me out of the picture so you can feel safe. So…I'll tell you what…stop looking for me, and I'll get out of your way. Is that a deal?"

"What makes you think I'm out to get rid of you? I just want you to be in a place that's out of danger. Can you understand that?"

"Oh, I understand what you're saying. It's just that I don't trust you."

"Simmons, that hurts. After all we've been through together, how can you say that?"

"Oh, I don't know, Chief. I'm only going on past history with you. I know you, so don't forget that I know what you're capable of. Remember, I've been there with you, and I know all the secrets."

"Okay, okay, but don't do anything foolish…just go."

"You got that right, Chief. And, don't you do anything foolish either. You should know that by now. I saw you at the cabin, and I saw how agitated you were. Don't ever believe that I'm not the kind to do foolish things. I've been paid well, and like I said, I'm out of here. And, just so you are aware, if I ever see you again, I will shoot you on the spot…So, adios, Chief."

He hung up the phone, took out the battery, and hurled the phone as far as he could, then crunched the battery under his boot. He mounted his bike and rode off.

Chief Lewis saw a cloud of dust far up in the hills and breathed a sigh of relief as he drove back to town in the opposite direction.

Chapter Ninety-Six

From a great vantage point, Lew watched the Chief circle the cabin. How he happened to be where he was did not surprise him, as his fogs had put him in places he could not imagine. This time, he found himself a little ways out of town in a field about one hundred feet west of the cabin in a copse of trees. His eyes adjusted to the change from fog to reality in time to observe the goings on at the cabin.

He observed the chief and his cell phone. As he gazed about, he spotted another man hidden from the chief also on a cell phone. He recognized him as Officer Simmons.

Though he could not hear the exchange between the two, he noticed the angry outburst from the chief before he got into his car and drove off.

His attention was drawn to where Simmons had stood. He saw him throw an object far to his right before climbing on a motorcycle and roaring off, causing a minor dust storm in his wake.

Lew watched until he could not see the bike anymore. He then strode over to the area where he believed the thrown object that Simmons had launched had landed.

When he reached the area, he saw a glint of shiny metal. He stopped, and as he looked down, a cell phone partially covered with grass was sitting with its chrome back shining in the sun. He carefully picked it up by its side, so as not to smudge any fingerprints that might be imprinted on it.

Slowly, he made it back to the road and as he reentered his fog state, he disappeared from view.

Chapter Ninety-Seven

"Ralph," Alan rushed up to his desk a little breathless, "You won't believe what Lew Wallace just brought in."

"I hope it's worthy enough to warrant you rushing in and out of breath to boot, Alan. What is it the Lew has?"

"I think he and we just broke the case. At least, that's what Lew thinks, and I tend to agree with him."

"Okay, Gina," Ralph called to her "Come on over and let's see just what Alan and Lew think they've got."

As Gina sashayed over to Ralph's desk, he watched as she smiled at him in her special way. His heart, as it had done many times before, somehow managed to skip a beat.

"You have to know that I did this, I mean, I found this when I was away, if you get my drift. It took me a little ways out of town, and I observed Chief Lewis and Officer Simmons, although they were never together. They communicated by this." He pointed to the cell phone he held gingerly by its sides.

"The chief was trying to get into a cabin out there, and Simmons was on a hill about 50 yards away, watching through a pair of binoculars. You can pull up their conversation if you have a battery. There isn't one in the phone right now. I saw Simmons throw this away and take off on his motorcycle, heading west. I hope this helps."

"Lew, I don't know what to say. You have given us a great leg up on this entire investigation and a big step in solving just what's going on here in Arthur. Thanks so much," Ralph said as he grasped Lew's shoulder and shook his hand.

The look on Lew's face was one of pride mixed with a touch of embarrassment as he took this sort of praise...not well.

"I just hope it turns out to be a good thing, really," he said as he started to back out of the room, trying to hide his discomfort with the praise, as he always did.

"Please, Lew, don't leave. You're part of this team now, and we want you to be with us until the finish. Isn't that right guys?" Ralph said as he slipped a spare battery into the back of the phone.

"Okay, let's see what we have here." he said.

For about ten minutes they all sat, while the memory ran on to disclose the conversation of Lewis and Simmons.

"Wow", Gina was the first to speak up, "This is so incriminating. How do we want to handle it? It's not the FBI's problem unless some federal laws have been broken, but I guess I can help out with your jurisdiction until something turns up for my guys."

"Gina, we would appreciate any help you give us, and I can speak for Ralph who seems speechless just now. We welcome everything and anything you can do with whatever."

"You got it guys", she said and looked over at Ralph, who just sat there looking like a person in a trance state.

"Ralph, are you just going to sit there and not say anything?"

"Alan, Gina, I'm stunned, really shaken. I thought Lewis was a stand-up guy. He gave us so much help it doesn't make sense, unless he's that good an actor. Like I said, I'm stunned."

"Well, I guess he is", Alan said, as he looked over at Gina, "What do you think?"

"I've known some sociopaths that look like saints, but would and did such horrible things, and no one ever suspected them, and to this day they could pass among us like nothing ever happened. This will not be an easy thing to convince people here that Lewis is the man behind it all…We need a confession."

Alan and Ralph both nodded their heads in agreement.

"The problem is…to persuade Lewis to do that."

"Right," the two detectives said simultaneously as they turned the cell phone back on and listened again to the damning conversation.

Chapter Ninety-Eight

Chief Lewis in the meantime was sitting across from the Mayor's desk in full uniform regalia, his medals shining in the morning sun.

"Mayor, I think the motorcycle gang situation has been completely disbanded and is over. The gangs have moved on and our streets are quiet and safe again. Do you think we still need the NYPD detectives? Are they really necessary anymore?"

"Well, Chief, you seemed to have handled the whole thing with your usual professionalism. Let me talk to the cops and see how they want to handle their end. I'll talk to them this morning and let you know how it pans out."

He stood to his 5' 5" stature, extended his hand, and warmly shook the chief's hand.

"I'll let you know this afternoon, okay?"

"Okay, Your Honor, glad to be of service. Let me know if you need anything else."

The chief strode confidently out of the Mayor's office, nodded to the secretary, and more or less paraded the few doors down to the station house, thinking he was home free.

He sat behind his big desk, put his feet to rest on the bottom drawer, and breathed a deep sigh of relief.

"Man, it doesn't get better than this." he said to himself, not knowing that the axe was soon to fall on his burly neck.

He sifted through some innocuous papers on his desk while the three people who were about to topple his inflated world opinion of himself were on their way to his office.

Chapter Ninety-Nine

"We have to tread very lightly here guys. Lewis is not a stupid man, after all. He's been running this department for a lot of years," Gina said as she ran her finger down a sheet of figures.

"He appears to be adjusting some of the statistics with regards to crimes of a serious nature to make it seem that he has done a very good job for the town. If he's making a run at the Mayor's job he is pumping up his record," she added "That, and with the money he recovered from the bikers over the years he's got to have a huge war chest."

"Once the people hear about his criminal doings and the fact that he's the one behind all the crap that's been going on here, I think they'll be close to hanging him, instead of electing him Mayor."

"Well, we have the cell phone recording. That should be enough to sink his hopes, as well as charge him with conspiracy, at least, if not outright murder," Alan said icily.

"We don't have time to bring this to the attention of the mayor or the city council. We have to act…now!!!" Ralph said as he prepared to storm into Chief Lewis's office.

"Ralph, wait," Gina said, "I have a federal warrant coming down in about a half an hour. We should wait for that before barging in there and possibly jeopardizing our case."

"But, Gina, he could be preparing either to making a break or destroying incriminating evidence", said the grim-faced detective.

"I'll tell you what, why don't I just go in friendly like and sit down and start an inane conversation with him. You know, just a delaying tactic. What do you think?" Gina asked.

"Might work," Alan said, "Why not try it, but you've got to be very careful. He's a good actor, as we well know. If he tries anything we'll be right outside."

She arose and approached the Chief's office door. She reached out and knocked lightly.

The Chief's voice, just as lightly called out, "Who is it?"

He sounded very stressed, but Gina responded sweetly, "It's just me, Gina. Can I come in, sir?"

Seconds elapsed before his voice responded, "Of course, do come in, Agent Grant."

Tentatively, Gina opened the door, not expecting to find what appeared to be the mere shadow of the robust man they had been used to seeing. His entire frame had somehow seemed to have shrunken. His uniform, that had been his pride and joy, that he had filled out fully, looked like it had become too large for him.

"Er, Chief, do you have a few moments for me?"

"Well, I am quite busy right now. Is it important or can it wait?"

"Well," she hesitated slightly feigning hesitancy, "I do have one or two things that my SAC (senior agent in charge) wanted me to talk to you about. But, if you're too busy, I guess it can wait. But, he did seem sort of insistent when he spoke to me just before."

"Oh, well, if it's that important. I guess I can't hold up the FBI now, can I?"

"Actually, it's about a theory that my SAC has presented to me about the murder across the county line."

"What murder across the county line? I haven't heard about any murder like that," he said, perspiration breaking out across his brow.

Gina was stalling and she knew that the thing she just thought up would keep him busy for more than enough time for the warrant to arrive. She also noticed his reaction when she mentioned a murder, he absolutely seemed quite shaken. It was as if she had caught him with something he thought he had gotten away with.

Stuttering slightly he said, "Agent Grant, is there anything else you want to talk about," he wanted her to get out of his office so he could think. "If not, I have an appointment that I have to be at right about now. So, if that's all, I'll take my leave and see you later."

The Chief stood. He rocked a little, regained his balance, and then escorted Gina to the door with a hand on the small of her back. She went back to her desk and reluctantly watched him leave.

Chapter One Hundred

"Ralph, we got him. The forensic guys have sent back the report. It's Lewis' voice and on Simmons' cell phone. This nails it down."

"Okay, but we still need to go slow. He's a very well respected man here in town. It's going to take a little tact and a lot of diplomacy to get the town council to back us. We need that warrant before we can make our move," Ralph said looking directly in Gina's eyes.

"It should be here any moment, Ralph. I'll make another call," she said as she went back to her desk. As she did, she happened to look out the window and observed Chief Lewis get in his personal car and tear out of the station's parking lot, kicking up stones and a lot of dust in his wake.

Gina called out, "Hey, I think the Chief's making a break for it, he just left in what appears to be a huge hurry."

"Call downstairs to the desk. Alert them that a suspect is fleeing the scene--don't mention any names. But, have them alert the cruisers and put out a BOLO (be on the lookout) for his car, add on -do not apprehend- just follow along order for now," Ralph said to Alan as he retrieved his Sig Saur automatic from his desk drawer. He checked the load and engaged the safety before he placed it in his shoulder holster.

"We can't wait for that warrant. Let's go guys."

The three left the squad room after Gina and Alan adjusted their weapons to their liking.

Stopping at the front desk, the sergeant waved a blue envelope at Ralph. It was the much awaited and much needed arrest warrant.

On the run, Ralph plucked it out of the sergeant's outstretched hand and pushed out the side door going directly to the car.

"ATTENTION ALL CRUISERS, A BLUE FORD CROWN VICTORIA IS HEADING WEST AND IS BEING FOLLOWED BY OFFICER URBAN NEEDS TO BE STOPPED AND THE DRIVER TAKEN INTO CUSTODY. THIS IS A BOLO ALERT AND ALL CARS ARE REQUIRED…OVER"

"Car 2, Roger."

"Car 3, Roger", were the replies, with no questions asked.

With Ralph at the wheel, Alan and Gina manned the GPS monitor.

Gina said, "He's still heading due west, and he's got at least a ten minute lead. Urban should be right on his tail by now."

"Unless he pulls off the road and takes a road that will through off Urban. The GPS doesn't lie, unless he knows how to disable it. If he does, we'll need a chopper to find him", Alan suggested in a strained voice.

"Let's not get too far ahead of ourselves, okay?"

"You got it, boss."

"And lose that BOSS remark. We're partners, no matter what the titles say. So, no boss, right?"

"Can I call you boss?"…Gina looked up and smiled with a glint of mischief in her eyes.

"You can call me anything you want, but let's concentrate on the job in front of us. You and I will discuss the other thing after."

"Yes, Boss", she countered, looking back at the monitor.

Alan pointed through the front windshield at a grouping of squad cars further up the road, "It looks like we have a 'go' here, get ready".

As they pulled up behind the last cruiser and started to open their doors, a shot rang out echoing in the stillness of the open road.

Ralph immediately pulled Gina down below the dashboard shouting, "Al, get down."

It was not necessary because Alan had already dropped to the floor of the back compartment.

"I hope they don't return fire," Ralph said of the three officers up ahead. "I'd like to take him in alive if possible."

No other shots were fired and Ralph breathed a sigh of relief.

Slowly he opened his door and stepped out with his hands showing, a clear indication he did not have his weapon out.

"Chief," he called out "Don't make this any worse than it already is. We're not going to shoot. We just want to talk to you. We can clear this up, put up your weapon, and come forward. No one will shoot you."

Officer Urban and the two other officers were looking at each other, wondering what the hell was going on. They did not put their weapons down and kept their eyes on Ralph as he talked to their chief.

"I don't believe you, Detective. I've been around a long time, and I know how this works, so forget about it."

"I'm not trying to scam you, Chief. I just don't want anybody to get hurt here, I want this to be over. So please…put your gun down, and let's talk."

"Good try, Bloom. But, you will have to come and get me and I promise it's not going to be easy…or pretty."

Ralph went up to the rear cruiser and spoke to Sam Urban.

"Sam, what do you think?"

"I think the Chief has his mind set. And, if I know the Chief, he has more than one weapon. I believe he has a riot gun in his car."

"Do you think he will use it, is the question?"

"If he's desperate enough, yes, and he's very good with it. I've seen him in action."

"Then you'd better get on the horn for more help. This could get very ugly."

"You got it, Detective," Urban said as he grasped the microphone to call it in.

Chapter One Hundred-One

Lew Wallace found himself on the road, he had emerged from the fog and in an instant, he saw the cars in the distance. There was a fourth car and he was standing directly in front of the grill of that vehicle. He recognized the Chief of Police facing the other cars with a gun in his hand. He was undecided as to what to do. All he knew was the Chief had just shot at the other cars, and there was tenseness about the situation.

He hesitated before moving, but his intention was to try to talk the Chief into putting down his weapon. How he was going to accomplish this, he had no idea.

He silently worked his way around the front of the car and stood directly behind the armed man. He was close enough to tap the chief on the shoulder, but instead he spoke in a soft, calm voice.

"Excuse me, Chief. Can I be of any help?"

The Chief reacted violently. He wheeled around, bringing the gun up and under Lew's chin.

"What the hell are you doing here? And how the hell did you get here?" he yelled in Lew's face.

Calmly Lew placed his right hand on the Chief's gun hand and eased it from under his chin saying, "Please, Chief, I'm only here to help. It's not necessary to point that thing at me."

He pointed to the gun that was shaking in the Chief's hand.

"I asked you how the hell you got here. I didn't hear or see a car, so how did you get here and what do you want?"

"How I got here isn't important. What is important is that I'm here to help you not make a bigger mistake by getting yourself or anybody else killed for no reason."

"If you take my advice you will get out of here the same way you got here, if you know what's good for you. And, there is a very good reason I'm here."

During this occurrence, Ralph and his team took the opportunity to move up to the lead cruiser where they observed the confrontation of Lew and the chief.

Alan and Gina shook their respective heads in confusion.

"Well, I'll be darned," Alan said.

Gina responded, "I wish he'd get his backside out of there. No telling what's on the Chief's agenda. He's going to get hurt."

Back at the Chief's car, Lew kept talking in his calm and soothing voice.

"Chief, this can all be settled without guns and you know it. Please put yours down and I'm sure they will put theirs down, also."

"Lew, I've given you a chance to get out of here, now I think you can help me. Put your hands up and stand in front of me."

Instead of complying, Lew lifted his right hand, in a flash grabbed the Chief's gun, and wrested it out of his hand.

"Wha, what the hell? How did you do that? Put that gun down and get out of the way," Chief stammered, unable to believe what just happened.

"Detectives," Lew called out, "You can come over now, the chief is ready to talk."

Instead of going along peacefully, Chief Lewis darted back into his car, grabbed the riot gun from its rack, and brought it to bear on Lew's back.

"Drop my gun, Lew, or I'll make a hole in your back large enough to drive this car through."

"Chief, don't do anything you'll be sorry for," Lew whispered.

"I've already done that. So, drop the gun…now"

This was the first time fear crept into Lew's mind. Not for himself, but for what would happen to his wife if he died this day. He dropped the gun on the road and slowly backed away.

Lewis picked up his handgun and quickly moved into the driver's seat, slammed the door, threw the car into gear, and roared off.

"Damn," Ralph sputtered, "What the hell just happened?"

"He's gone," Gina said, not believing her eyes.

Chapter One Hundred-Two

He muttered to himself as he roared off, "Damn, now, I've got to run. How did they catch on and how the hell did Lew Wallace get to me?"

The car rocketed back and forth kicking up dust and a bevy of roadside stones. He looked back through the rear view mirror and saw the five people scurrying around, pointing to his speeding car.

"If they don't get moving soon I've got a chance," he said to no one in particular, "My only hope is that they don't have the authority to order up a chopper."

Lew was gone as soon as Lewis took off. The fog had enveloped him just as it did when he arrived.

Gina looked around and said to Ralph, "Did you see Lew leave? And, how is it possible he got here without anyone seeing him? He had no car."

"I'll explain later, we have to get after him now. Call and see if we can get a helicopter in the air and out here."

"I've already called my AC (agent in charge). He said it will be here ASAP."

"Good, let's see if we can keep him in sight. It looks like his car has more under the hood than we have. The only thing is not to let him get too far ahead of us now."

At this, the three climbed into their car and sped off in Lewis's direction, leaving the three cruisers sitting on the road and the officers in complete disbelief.

Urban looked at his officers and said, "Jeez, I don't believe it. The Chief is in the run. I wonder what they have on him to make him take off and to shoot at us to boot?"

The other officers just shrugged their shoulders and said nothing. They just stared after the speeding cars.

"I guess I'll call this in," Urban said, scratching his head in confusion.

In the meantime, Lew had arrived back in Arthur. His wife, Linda, looked at him with curiosity as he walked into the house.

She asked, "Well, Lew, what happened? You've only been gone a short time. Did you get done what you needed to do?"

"Yes, I guess so. The rest is up to the detectives. They're chasing the Chief down. I can only hope they catch him."

He sighed heavily and plopped down in his favorite armchair.

"It's getting more difficult to do what I did. This time it took a lot out of me. It doesn't seem to be as smooth a process anymore, if you know what I mean."

"I'm sorry Lew, but you know you don't have to do this," she said.

"I know, but sometimes I can't help it, I wish I could."

She looked at her husband with such love in her eyes that one tear fell from her right eye.

"Take it easy now, dear," she said and went to brew him his favorite tea. Looking back at him, seeing his eyes close, and breathing lightly, as if a burden had been lifted.

Chapter One Hundred-Three

"This is Police Helicopter Unit 2. We're 30 miles out of Arthur. We're following the Chief's Chrysler 500 at about 3,000 feet. He's heading west, traveling at 75 miles per hour. I don't think he knows we're up here yet, but it's only a matter of time 'til he catches on."

"Roger that, Number 2, stay on him. It doesn't matter if he sees you. He's probably monitoring the radio in his vehicle, so he knows we're after him. Over."

"Roger, that. We'll stay for a long as our fuel holds out."

Ralph, Alan, and Gina heard these transmissions as they sped after Lewis. No one said a word for long time, but their intense looks betrayed their feelings.

Gina broke the eerie silence and said, "I can't believe he fooled all of us. I, myself, believed he had only the best intentions for the town."

"Yes, well, power has a way of seducing people. Even good people," Ralph said as his hands gripped the wheel even tighter.

"But, Ralph, he was a good cop. Even in the city he was a top candidate to move up the chain of command," she said.

"Something must have happened that no one in the department would talk about. When we get back, it's something to look into."

"Yeah…something…" Alan muttered.

A glint of silver tweaked Ralph's eyes, "Look out," he shouted as he swerved the car onto the shoulder of the road.

They felt the impact of a high-powered bullet hitting the rear of their car before they actually heard the shot.

"It's a lucky thing you saw him, Ralph. He missed me by inches," Alan said a little breathlessly, as they all piled out the opposite side of the car, each pulling their weapons, and disengaging the safeties.

Ralph had the foresight to take a megaphone from the squad room before they left. He raised it to his lips and pressed the send button.

"Chief," he called out after the initial squawk of the phone, "Chief," he repeated, "You've got nowhere to go. We don't want any more firing. Put down the rifle and come out. We don't want anyone hurt here."

"Don't kid me, Detective. You know you have to take me in and I can't allow you to do that. I'd rather die out here than go to jail, you get me?" Lewis shouted out, taking another shot at their car.

"Chief," Ralph said over the megaphone, "It doesn't have to be that way. Agent Grant can get you in a federal facility and you will be under the FBI's program. Think about it."

"No, you think about this", Lewis yelled out and put his next bullet through the detective's windshield, glass imploding inside the car.

A loud thudding descended on the location. The Police chopper was coming down behind the Chief's car. As he looked up, his attention was diverted long enough for the three behind their car to quickly rush across the 50 yards separating the two cars and arrive weapons at the ready alongside the Chief's Chrysler.

Chief Lewis directed his attention back to their car, not aware that they were already in his proximity.

While the chopper pilot called out to him to drop his weapon, he shook his head and motioned them away.

When he did this, Alan rose up from behind him. Ralph stood up, and aimed his Glock directly at his heart.

Gina, in the meantime, gingerly stood up from the other side of the Chrysler's hood and trained her service weapon at his head.

"I think that sometimes you have to realize that your intentions and dreams have been just that…dreams, Chief. Please drop your weapon."

The chief looked from one officer to another, their weapons all pointed at him. The chopper pilot also had his weapon trained at him. A look of utter disbelief and defeat crossed his rugged face, his shoulders suddenly sagged. This 6'2", 215 lb. formerly robust man appeared to shrivel before their eyes, until there appeared a miniscule spark in his otherwise sad eyes.

Instead of dropping the riot gun, his body shuddered and he either voluntarily or possibly involuntarily brought it up to bear on Ralph, as his finger groped for the trigger.

Alan, Gina, and Ralph all recognized what was about to happen and simultaneously, they fired.

The sound echoed across the empty road as if a thunderstorm had let loose a powerful clap.

The Chief had been hit in three different places. For a brief moment, his body stood straight up, before slowly crumbling forward. The life that had formally been in his eyes went out as his body fell heavily to the ground.

Gina ran around the front end of the car and stood with Ralph, their guns still smoking.

"Oh, dear, why did he have to do that, Ralph?"

"I guess he didn't want to go to jail or have his life opened up to public scrutiny. He didn't want to be held in contempt by everyone in town."

"Well, that's exactly what's going to happen anyway. They will crucify him in their hearts."

"I guess so," she said.

Chapter One Hundred-Four

Officer Sam Urban, being the senior officer at the department, sat behind Chief Lewis's desk poring over all the paperwork engendered by the recent events. His cheeks puffed out with the enormity of the pile.

Sam, as acting chief, had experienced a nearly sleepless night, thinking about what faced him in the morning. His wife of three years had sat up and watched him through the night, tossing and turning in their bed.

Now that he sat there, in the seat of authority, he was wide-awake and if not anxious, he was prepared to do what was necessary to get the job done.

Ralph, Alan, and Gina sat in front of his desk and provided Acting Chief Urban with all the evidence they had gathered pertaining to Lewis' dealings.

"Okay, guys," Sam said, "I think I've gotten all the information that I need. The District Attorney has signed off on the case and there doesn't seem like there's anything else for you to do. Your testimony and the papers we found in his desk were enough to prove he was responsible for all that happened here, from the bikers to the break-ins and the arrangements for the killings. I guess you all can get back to the city with our gratitude for a job well done. I personally thank you for everything you did."

With this, he rose and shook hands all around.

The trio left the office, collected their belongings, and prepared to leave. Unfortunately, the entire squad of Arthur's peace officers and the Mayor detained the three with huge smiles plastered across their faces. The Mayor stepped forward with his hand held out.

"Detectives, the entire town has gotten together and we want to thank you for your services. The good citizens of Arthur didn't know just how to show their appreciation until I thought that the key to the city would be the only way to properly thank you. So, if and when you ever feel you would like to come back to Arthur, we will welcome you with our hearts wide-open," and with this the Mayor held out an oversized gold plated key, emblazoned with the seal of Arthur on its blade.

Ralph accepted the key on behalf of the three of them, and haltingly thanked them in as few words as he could. He was not accustomed to speaking off the cuff, unless it pertained to police matters.

That done the three of them loaded themselves into their car and, amid waves from everyone, drove out of town, heading for the city.

At the back of the crowd, a lone man stood. He wanted to thank the trio personally, but being the private person that he was, he felt that it would not be proper to make that display.

Instead, Lew Wallace executed a smart salute to the three that had placed their

confidence in him and for which he came
through.

Chapter One Hundred-Five

Back in the city, and after briefing the Chief of
Detectives, they retired to their desks to write
their final reports.

Ralph approached Gina's desk, and after
his stammering for a few moments, she looked
up and said, "Ralph, what are you trying to say?"

"Er, I mean, um, er, Gina, you know I'm
no good at this stuff", he finally said.

"Yes, Ralph. I know."

"So, where are you going now?" he asked
while twisting a piece of scrap paper in his
perspiring hands.

"Well, where do you think I should go,
Ralph?"

"I, er, think I would like you to stay here
with me. I mean, please don't go back to DC," he
finally blurted out.

"But, Ralph, you know I'm FBI and my
job requires that I go back there. We've gone
through this before. You know that they've
offered you a job with them and it would be in
DC with me," Gina said, as she looked deep in
Ralph's eyes.

"Right, I remember. But, I'm a New York cop, I wouldn't really fit in with the suits in DC. You know I wouldn't fit in there, don't you?"

"Yes, Ralph, I do. And, that's why I have to go back and tender my resignation. I want to be with you, Ralph. I love you and I want to share my life with you." she said this as she watched his face change from bleak to the biggest grin she had ever seen on it ever.

"You mean, I mean, you're not fooling with me, are you? You're going to quit the Bureau and come here to me?" he said, unable to keep the happiness from bubbling to the surface.

He rushed around her desk and grabbed her up in the gentlest bear hug he could manage in his glee.

"Alan," he shouted to his partner, "Did you hear? She's staying with me, I mean us. Can you believe it?"

Alan gave him a thumbs-up and looked at his partner, not believing the happiness he saw in his otherwise implacably stoic face.

"Gina, I have to ask, when did you come to the decision?"

"Oh," she said feigning boredom, until she broke out in a broad smile "From the first day I was assigned to be on your team, you big boob. Tell me you didn't know?"

"How could I know?" he asked with a smile that was as wide as hers was.

"You're so naïve, and …so…sweet," she said as she planted an enormous kiss on his smiling lips.

Ralph just stood there, his face bright red, but with a huge smile on it.

The end…"possibly."

Chick Gallin Tetralogy

Anything: An American Mystery

An intrepid New York detective is on the chase of his life, crisscrossing the US from New York to the borders of Canada and Mexico and back. Meanwhile, David North is fascinated with the woman he spoke to briefly on the ferry. Who is she, and why did she implicate him in a murder that has cops chasing a stone-cold killer across the country? Not to mention, how is he supposed to get her spellbinding beauty off his mind? Join author Chick Gallin in this compelling crime thriller that has lives intersecting in ways only fate can orchestrate and killers meeting their match in a chase that grips readers from page one. Anything can happen.

Nothing

Follow the NYPD, FBI, and the Department of Defense while they mount an all-out search for a band of relentless killers hired by an international syndicate to invade homes of high-level executives and steal their top-secret information. The intrepid detectives of the NYPD combined with a beautiful FBI agent have no leads until a young victim provides vital clues that bring down not only the band of killers but also the syndicate itself. The exciting climax will leave the readers wanting more.

Something

A fog, a hometown hero, a motorcycle gang war, three veteran detectives in a small town, and the problems that have to be rectified before that town is at peace again. As Detective Ralph Bloom was saying to his partner Detective Alan Beckman and Special FBI Agent Gina Grant, "Something very strange is happening in Arthur".

Everything 📱

Ride along with Detectives Ralph Bloom and his erstwhile partner Alan Beckman and the beautiful FBI Agent Gina Grant as they hunt for the sadistic bomber plaguing New York City's citizens and streets. No one was prepared for the explosive conclusion of this one of a kind case.

Chick Gallin, Author

Chick Gallin served in the Korean Conflict, the New York Fire Department, and was a private investigator in the South Florida area. He authored the tetralogy of **Anything, Nothing, Something,** *and* **Everything.**